LIFE *with* BINGO

JIM BLACK & JIM LEWIS

outskirts press

Outskirts Press, Inc.
http://www.outskirtspress.com

Paperback ISBN: 978-1-9772-4024-8

Cover design by Probook Premade Book Covers @ www.premade-bookcovers.com All rights reserved - used with permission.

Outskirts Press and the "OP" logo are trademarks belonging to Outskirts Press, Inc.

PRINTED IN THE UNITED STATES OF AMERICA

For Max and Scoot Black
We'll see you again at the Rainbow Bridge
—J.B.

To Jim for allowing me to come along

To Karen for putting up with all of my insanity
To Teff and Sean for giving me purpose
And to Kristina and Garrett,
Lighthouses with bright beacons
—J.L.

ACKNOWLEDGEMENTS

Our sincere thanks to:

Barbara Rhyne and Tom Hoffman, PhD, for their valuable suggestions and aid in helping us whip our manuscript into shape.

Milos and the crew at Probook Premade Book Covers for their beautiful work.

Jamie, Elaine and everyone at Outskirts Press for putting it all together in such grand fashion.

And finally, to the Bingos and Johns of this world:
Our thoughts and prayers are with you all.

PROLOGUE

His name is Bingo.

That's all—no last name. He's sixteen years old, sort of skinny with short brown hair and a killer smile he hasn't had a lot of chances to use until now. Most would say life has dealt him a pretty tough hand, but you won't hear him fret or complain. He's over it. He has been ever since he found the tree with feelings and started seeing things differently. You see, Bingo finally learned it's all about the choices we make. And because of those he's made, things are good now. And getting better. And with me at his side, he'll *always* know what it's like to be loved. How many people can really say that? Not nearly as many as you think, I bet.

If you've got time on your hands, we'll tell you our story. How we got from Center, Texas, to Kalispell, Montana. And all the stuff that happened in between.

I guess I should warn you that some of it is kind of sad. But a lot isn't. In the end you'll be smiling, I promise. Just like me. Except your tongue probably won't be hanging out like mine. My name's John. I'm a dog.

But not just any dog. I'm the luckiest dog on the planet. I'm Bingo's dog. And not by happenstance either. I believe I was put here for a reason. You see, everyone should have a best-friend-for-life dog. And a great many people do or at least know someone who does. But some need one more than others. And Bingo was pretty high on that list when I came along.

Just so you know, I'm what you might call an orange mutt. My mom was a terrier of some sort and I never knew my dad. (Humans aren't the only ones with worthless fathers who just up and leave.) Whatever he was, I wound up with his crooked ears and his crooked tail. And I'm not a big dog—residing somewhere just south of medium I guess you could say—but big enough.

I'm also intuitive, clear-thinking and wise beyond my seven years. At least I like to think I am. And those traits have served me well. Especially during our recent adventure on the open road. But enough about me. I want you to know all about Bingo. What kinda guy he is. What he's been through. And just how big his dadgum heart is. Now, if you happen to be one of those who doesn't care much for the sentimental stuff, there's plenty of adventure too. Together, he and I have seen a lot of things, had our share of close calls and have met some *real* interesting people. So let's get started. Whatta you say?

CHAPTER 1

JOHN

Bingo was born at 7:00 p.m. on Groundhog Day in 2003 at Warren Hospital in Center, Texas. Now, you'd think that Center, Texas, would be somewhere near the middle of the Lone Star State, but it's really way out in East Texas near the Louisiana border. So answer me this: If a town doesn't even know where it belongs, how's a kid that's born there ever supposed to? Anyway, it'd been sleeting for two days straight, and everything was covered with an inch of solid ice. His daddy wasn't there to see him born. Not because the roads were bad, but because Joel Bookman didn't want no damn baby and stayed home watching a fishing show on TV instead. Anyway, about Bingo's name. When the time came to fill out the birth certificate, his mother was scared to give him her husband's last name and didn't want to use her maiden name because she felt he deserved better. Other than her beautiful son, the only thing she had to show for her life was a string of bad choices. So she just left it blank. When they got home the next night, Joel wouldn't hold him or hardly look at him. He did ask what his name was. When Lily told him, he looked at her like she's crazy and asked why the hell she'd name him a stupid thing like that. She said it was because she was always lucky playing bingo, and hoped the name might bring *him* luck. He told her she was nuts because if that was the case, she shoulda named him Crapped Out cause that's what they call it when you lose at dice and she was a loser, plain and simple.

Lily Bookman was a good mom. She didn't do the right thing in the end, but Bingo will tell you she tried hard. Fear can cripple people (even us dogs), and years of living with Joel had left her an invalid of sorts. With Joel around, she was Night—dark and quiet. When he was gone, she was Day—bright and full of hope. Bingo liked Day best, but those times were few and far between. And when Joel drank, which was often, life in their little house was downright scary. He was mean when he drank. Bingo got his first real spanking on his first birthday (for getting a small dab of cake frosting on Joel's shirt), and as he got older the spankings got harder and more frequent. By seven, they weren't spankings anymore. Bingo was getting slapped. And punched. And worse. Occasionally, in a rage, Joel would cover Bingo's mouth and nose with his hand so he couldn't breathe, telling him if he screamed or kicked and fought he was a sissy, and sissies didn't deserve to live because they were usin' up space and air that braver, more deservin' people needed. Then, at the last instant, he'd release his hold just before Bingo passed out. But not always.

Lily felt powerless to do anything. Sometimes she watched in horror, but most times she retreated to the carport and sat in their Ford pickup with the radio turned up loud. Still, Bingo not once looked at her actions (or lack of) as meaning she didn't love him. She did and he knew it. And he loved her.

As bad as the physical hurt was, Bingo always managed to survive and heal. Try as he may, though, he just wasn't able to recover from the emotional beatings. If he'd had just one, single happy memory of his dad to hold onto, things might have been different. But he didn't. Not one. Something had to change.

CHAPTER 2

BINGO

I t was going to be a long walk home. It was always a long walk home, but it was going to be even longer today. There was going to be hell to pay. Coming home early would require an explanation—an explanation I did not want to have to give. But, oddly, instead of the knot in my stomach and the fear that I usually felt, today there was just resignation. I was more tired than afraid and just disgusted with it all. I guess there comes a time in every life when people finally just get fed up. I had just gotten fired at the small hardware store where I worked. Two kids playing in the store had knocked over a big display of Christmas ornaments Mr. Edgars, the owner, had erected despite it being summer because he loved Christmas so much. The broken pieces were lying all over the floor. I was trying desperately to clean them up when he walked around the corner to see what the commotion was about. He immediately assumed I was responsible and began yelling at me, "You stupid kid! What have you done now? You're fired! Get out and don't come back!" I guess I had just had it up to here with people telling me how inadequate I was and how I was never going to amount to anything.

I didn't exactly have an idyllic home life. My dad seemed to love the bottle way more than he loved us. He was bitter about every single thing that life had dealt him, and his rage was always just below the surface ready to erupt at any moment. My mom tried, but I guess that she had lived in fear for so long that she had just been beaten down. There just didn't seem to be much left inside her. As for me, I had just turned sixteen. I was still awkward and gangly and painfully shy, but I was starting to fill out a little bit and Dad no longer seemed so overwhelming. But mostly, I was just tired. And fed up.

When I walked in the door, there was already trouble brewing. Dad was screaming at Mom, a far too often occurrence, about the light bill. It was $25 higher than last month's and he was livid. The same old nonsense about how he worked his tail off to support us and how ungrateful we were and how we just wasted everything. As soon as he heard the door shut he turned on me. "What the hell are you doing home early? Get your butt back to that store and earn some money."

"I got fired," I said quietly.

He grabbed me by the shirt and threw me into the couch. Then he was on top of me, slapping me and hitting me. "You are worthless!" he screamed, "just another ungrateful, useless mouth I have to feed. You and that stupid dog! I'm gonna kill that dog right now."

"That dog" was the only true friend I had ever had, and he was completely innocent in all of this. When Dad said that, something snapped. I unconsciously grabbed the big glass ashtray off the table. All the years of fear and anger and wearing long sleeves in the summer to hide the bruises, and the hurtful remarks about being such a klutz and the frustration with never letting anyone my age get close to me came boiling to the surface. I swung the ashtray at him as hard as I could, striking him square on the jaw. He had a puzzled look on his face for a moment and then fell straight to the floor. I did not even think about checking to see if he was okay. I grabbed Mom and said, "Come on. Now is our chance. Let's get out of here!" She pulled away.

"Honey, I can't go," she cried. "I can't leave."

I knew that no amount of pleading was going to change her mind, so I rushed to my room and threw my school books out of my backpack and onto the floor. I wasn't going to need them anymore. I grabbed as many clothes as I could and stuffed them into the backpack. I had nearly a hundred dollars stashed away that I had hidden from Dad, and I grabbed that too. I threw on my cap and headed outside to get John. "Bye, Mom" was all I said.

I hesitated for just a moment when John and I got to the end of the sidewalk. I vaguely remembered an old song or poem about where the sidewalk ends and the road begins. I looked down at my only friend. "Well, buddy, we have nowhere to go. But we sure can't stay here." So we stepped off the curb together and I said, "Let's go to the mountains. I have always wanted to see a mountain."

And so we were off. I knew that the road ahead might become pretty desperate, but I also knew that it couldn't possibly be worse than the way things were at home. Thankfully, I had the only living creature I had ever been able to trust right beside me. We started walking into the setting sun.

CHAPTER 3

―――

JOHN

―――

Joel Bookman didn't allow dogs in his house, so I was relegated to the confines of the tiny back yard where I spent several freezing winters and blazing summers with only a hastily built make-shift doghouse for shelter. That's all Joel would allow. But Bingo kept me fed, watered and loved. What else does one need?

I was lying in the shade of the porch when I heard the commotion. It was not an unfamiliar sound. Usually, Bingo came out and sat with me following one of their confrontations—often with cuts, scrapes or worse. As much as I wanted to tear into Joel, Bingo wouldn't allow it. "No good will come of it, buddy. He'll take you far out in the country and dump you on the side of an old dirt road. Or worse. And I can't lose you. Try and understand."

I did. If Bingo only knew I understood his every word. But he didn't. And I had no way of telling him.

Whatever went on that day was different however. Bingo hadn't sat beside me. Or knelt. Rather, he just said, "Come on, boy. We're leaving." It was then I noticed the backpack on his back. Were we really leaving? Was that possible? I sure hoped so. The little house located at 2410 Sycamore

―――

Street was not a happy place.

We walked several blocks before stopping at an Allsup's. Summer was in full swing and it was hot. I waited outside while Bingo went in. Shortly he returned with a handful of bottled waters, a paper cup and a small sack of other items. He stuffed everything into his backpack but for one water, which he opened. He poured some into the cup and held it out for me. I took a good long drink and looked up at him.

"It's gonna be fine, John, We're gonna be fine. Are you done?"

I barked. He smiled, rubbed my head, took a drink from the bottle and re-capped it. He then placed it in his backpack and said, "Let's go."

CHAPTER 4

BINGO

John and I spent that first night on a roadside park bench just outside of town. The day's heat was fading and the sky was clear. We were lucky. After a supper of cheese crackers and water, we settled in. I will admit the park bench was a little hard and I woke up a little stiff, but all in all it wasn't too bad. In fact, lying there looking at the stars was quite freeing and relaxing. Maybe I should have been scared sleeping out in the open like that, but I had been sleeping with one eye open for most of my life. Fear at bedtime was nothing new to me. And I trusted John to give me a warning growl if anything or anybody came too close.

As soon as I got stretched enough to move and awake enough to be aware, John started giving me that pleading look. He was hungry. I think this is when the enormity of my situation began to dawn on me. I was responsible for *two* lives. I had a little less than $100 hidden in a few places in my backpack and on me and little food and no prospects. I thought of returning to Center to buy more supplies, but I wasn't going back or looking back. Ever. We were going to go forward. I pulled out a couple of Slim Jims. They were gone in a flash and I stood.

"Come on, buddy." I said. And we were off. John looked a little disappointed, but I trusted that he was with me no matter what. For the first time, I felt the burden of being solely responsible for another life and vowed that I would never let John down. I tried to act jolly and confident, but John was smart and perceptive and I am sure he saw right through my act. In fact, I was pretty worried about what lay ahead and know he was too.

We had the morning sun to our backs, and soon the sun's heat was on us. We walked all morning before spotting a gas station up ahead. Before going in we went around back to a woefully neglected bathroom. There was no hot water and no soap, but I washed my face and rinsed my hair and cleaned up the best that I could. There were several rolls of toilet paper on top of the commode, and I helped myself to one and stuck it in my backpack. I bought a not very appetizing looking sausage sandwich, some trail mix, pork and beans and more bottled water. I hoped that would sustain us for a while. John and I shared the sandwich. That seemed to brighten his mood a little bit. Then we hit the road again.

The traffic was not too bad. It was mostly eighteen-wheelers, ranchers and farmers in pickups pulling livestock trailers, and an occasional oil field truck. Nobody offered a ride. What we needed was a Walmart or something where I could get a toothbrush and a few things like that. Things that I never even thought about when I rushed out the door. This being an adult and being responsible was not nearly as fun and exciting as I had imagined it to be.

We walked for most of the afternoon. I was careful that we took a little break every hour or so. I knew this was going to be a marathon and not a sprint. We had to use everything we had—energy, money, food and clothing—sparingly and wisely. The day was plenty warm. The land was lush and green and full of trees, mostly towering pines. Cattle roamed everywhere and pump jacks bobbed up and down in clearings between the trees. Cattle and oil were important to the local economy. When one or the other went bad, everybody suffered.

Before we knew it, the sun was low in the west sky and we were in the middle of nowhere. I spotted a small cluster of trees off the road a ways and headed to it.

CHAPTER 5

JOHN

"We're here for the night, boy." This was no roadside park and that was fine with me. Instead, it was a little tank with some trees along one side. Bingo plopped down beneath them. After a quick look around and a pee, I joined him. It was getting hard to see as he pulled out a can of pork and beans. We ate them along with some more water and then he laid back, his hands behind his head. Above us, stars were arriving. And part of the moon. Something hopped into the water near us. I jumped up and growled.

"Probably just a frog, boy. It's okay."

Knowing he was probably right, I lay back down. Hidden from the highway, we were in our own little world. A world I loved. Didn't matter where it was, just that it was me and him together. I curled up beside him, and later when he was asleep, I nudged closer, my back hard against his, and could feel his heartbeat—my favorite feeling in the whole world. Bar none. We dogs don't cry. I'm not sure why that is, but we don't. We do have feelings, though. And the feeling coursing through me right then and there was more than love. It was the realization I'd found true meaning in my life. And purpose. I'd always been loyal to Bingo but this was more than that. I was now his keeper. His protector. Something I hadn't had the chance to do before now. And now he needed me more than ever. And I needed him.

This declaration was followed by sweet dreams of chasing rabbits and squirrels. There were none to be found in that tiny back yard in Center, but this was the wild. No telling what we might come across. My dream was ruined when I was awakened early the next morning to the sound of something I despise. *Thunder.* I can't explain it. I don't think it's ever harmed a hair on my body, but it scares the dickens outta me. I sat up and looked. Far in the distance I could see a dark line of storms and occasional lightning. And the distant sound of you-know-what.

"It's okay, boy. Just a little thunder."

Easy for you to say.

"And it's a long way off. Still, we'd better eat and get moving." He pulled out the Slim Jims and fifteen minutes later we were on the road again. An hour later, the sky had grown really dark. The storms were no longer in the distance. Thankfully, the thunder had all but stopped. The lightning too. But the threat of hard rain was evident, and it wasn't long before the first few large drops found us. Five minutes later we were soaked. It was raining hard when an old, faded blue pickup pulled up alongside us. The driver, an old fella with longish grey hair under a John Deere cap, reached over and rolled down the passenger window.

"If I didn't know better, I'd say the two of you could use a ride."

"We're good," Bingo replied. "Thanks, though."

"Well now, I believe your interpretation of good and mine differ. From here it appears you're soaked to the gills and the prospect for drying out is nowhere in sight. Now, that said, I am a harmless old man with a dry, warm, old pickup truck. And I am headed to my little abode just up the road where I plan to fix me a good old-fashioned hot breakfast in the dry, warm confines of my modest home. Sure you don't want to join me?"

Bingo smiled at the man, stared down the road through the rain and looked at me. I did not hesitate in barking. That all sounded dang good to me.

"Looks like someone knows a good deal when he hears one," he said, laughing.

Bingo smiled and said, 'Thank you. That's nice of you." He reached down and picked me up to place me in the bed.

"No sense in that! He can ride up here. Get in." He opened the door.

Bingo set me on the seat and climbed in. The man reached over and scratched my head.

"Howdy, fella. What might your name be?"

"John," Bingo replied, climbing in. "And I'm Bingo."

The man smiled big and said, "Well, I'm Alvin. My friends call me Al." He put the truck in gear and started down the road. "What'd the two of you do, swap names once upon a time?"

"No," Bingo smiled. "Those are our names."

"That so? Well, they're solid names, that's for sure. Now, if I was guessin', I'd say somebody is runnin' away from somethin'. And neither of you look the type to have broken any laws or be in that kind of trouble, so I'm thinkin' it's somethin' at home. Would I be right?"

Bingo turned and stared out his window.

"Fair enough. It's really none of my business, so we'll just leave it at that." He turned off the highway and started up a gravel road with corn fields on both sides.

"Are you a farmer?"

"Used to be. 'Fore I got old. Nowadays I just lease out my land."

Shortly, we pulled up in front of a small wooden house surrounded by large oak trees. Al parked the truck out front, climbed out and walked to the porch. We followed him in.

"You can do what you want, but if I was you, I'd take a hot shower and change into some dry clothes. I 'spect you've got some in that pouch of yours. Meanwhile, John and I'll fix breakfast."

Bingo hesitated and then looked down the hall.

"Second door on your right."

Bingo nodded and headed that way. I'd peed and shaken out before entering, so I was good. I followed Al into the kitchen and stretched out on a small rug out of his way. It wasn't long before the smell of fried eggs, bacon, toast and coffee filled the room. After our last two breakfasts, it was almost more than I could bear. We dogs have quite the sense of smell, you know.

"I don't have any dog food, John, so I reckon you'll just have to have what we're havin'."

That definitely called for a bark. A loud one. He chuckled and pulled some orange juice from the fridge. A few minutes later, Bingo appeared in clean jeans and a dry white T-shirt.

"Have a seat, son. We're ready as we're gonna be." I followed Bingo to a small wooden table near a window. Outside, the rain was really coming down. Hooray for Al. I watched him fill a large plate and set it down in front of me. This called for two loud barks. I tried my best to eat slow and make mine last, but there are things in this world that are just plumb out of a dog's control. A minute later, my plate was clean. Slimy, but clean. Bingo managed a little more self-control but not much. It wasn't long before his was gone as well.

Al smiled at him. "That went pretty fast."

"Thank you, That was *really* good."

"More? I can fix it."

"No sir. That was plenty. Thank you."

For a moment, Al ate in silence. Once he'd finished, he spoke. "I had a dog once. A golden retriever. Saved my life."

"Really? How?"

Al pushed his empty plate away and wiped his face with a cloth napkin. I thought I saw his eyes water.

"We lost our beloved Olivia when she was seventeen. Got in a car with the wrong friends on the wrong night. Driver lost control and all three passengers were thrown out and killed. Our daughter one of 'em. Then, a week later, I lost her mom to cancer. Betsy had been sick for over a year." Al paused, gathering himself. Clearly, he was a private and proud man, embarrassed to show his feelings. I noticed Bingo's own eyes had filled.

"I wasn't worth a hoot after that. One day, a friend of mine gave me the keys to his cabin in Colorado and made me go. Said the time there away from here would do me good. So would the scenery. He was right about the scenery. It was beautiful there. But my hurt didn't stay behind. Finally I just came on home. I couldn't figure out how to get out from under what I was feelin' and didn't see an end to it. As a result, I was havin' some real bad thoughts. Finally, one mornin' I just couldn't do it anymore."

CHAPTER 6

JOHN

"What happened?"

"I was about to do somethin' terrible when I heard a noise out on the porch. I peered through the blinds and there was this dog—just sittin' there lookin' out over the yard like he owned the place. Darn thing sat there all afternoon and never budged. That evenin' I took him some water and some chicken, and he was with me fifteen years."

"What was his name?"

Al smiled. His tough patch had passed. Bingo's too.

"Poppy."

"Poppy?"

"Yeah, Poppy," Al replied, with a big grin. "Don't ask me why. It was just the first thing that jumped into my head. And it stuck."

"Was Poppy a boy or a girl?"

"Boy," Al chuckled. "Hey, he didn't care. That dog loved me. I don't know why. And if he hadn't showed when he did, I don't know what would've happened."

"If you had him fifteen years, he had a good, long life."

Needless to say, I'm not a big fan of being reminded just

---

how short life is for us dogs. What's up with that anyway? And who came up with that *one human year equals seven dog years* business? Give me a break.

"Yes he did. And he wasn't a puppy when I got him. Then, one day when he was about twelve, I noticed him drinkin' more water than usual. All day long it seemed. I took him to the vet, and he determined Poppy had diabetes. Of all things. I later read somewhere that feeding a dog human food can cause it. Or contribute to it. Now, on that note, I just fed John here a big plate of it. And I 'spect he hasn't been eatin' much better on the road. So you need to get him a bag of dog food first chance you get. You hear? No need takin' chances with his health."

What? Dry dog food? Oh, man. I think I'd rather take my chances.

"I'll do that," Bingo said. "We've always fed him table scraps at home. I didn't know."

"Well now you do. And let me tell you, havin' to give Poppy insulin shots twice a day wasn't much fun. I sat him down and explained what I was gonna do and why and it was like he understood me. He was a real trooper. I never had a problem one."

Shots twice a day? Uh, maybe dry dog food won't be that bad after all. Just take some getting used to, that's all.

"I gave him those shots for three years. Then one day he wouldn't eat. Just laid in the same spot all day. When he did finally get up to go outside, he collapsed. I rushed him into town, and the vet discovered he had a large tumor on his liver and was bleeding inside. He explained there wasn't anything they could do for him. Then it hit me. *Poppy wasn't going home.* Doc asked if I'd like a moment of privacy, and I said yes. Once he was gone, I bent down and told Poppy how much I loved him. And that he was the reason I was still here. And that I was so sorry."

Al and Bingo were both crying now. And I wasn't feeling so good myself.

"And then he gathered what tiny bit of strength he had left and looked up at me. And with his eyes, he was telling me he understood. And that he loved me too. And he thanked me for taking such good care of him all those years."

Al paused, took a deep breath and wiped his eyes. "One of the hardest things I've ever done. When it was over, I brought him home. He's buried out back under a redbud tree. I go out and talk to him every single day."

Bingo gathered himself and asked, "Did you ever get another dog?"

"No, son. I didn't."

Al stood and walked to the window and looked out. "Rain's let up some, but it's not over. Don't reckon I can convince the two of you to stay? At least for a day or two till the weather improves?"

Bingo gave it some thought and answered, "Thank you, Al. I know John'd be happy to but, well, I really want to get as far from Center as I can. As quick as I can. So I think we'll hit the road. I hope you understand."

Al smiled. "I do."

We watched as he walked into the kitchen and removed a couple of items from a cookie jar atop the refrigerator. He placed them in his jeans pocket and said, "Grab your belongin's and come with me."

CHAPTER 7

JOHN

W e followed him out the back door to an old barn. He opened a padlock and pulled the doors open wide. There sat something under an old filthy tarp. It was too big to be a bicycle and too small to be a car. He pulled the tarp away with a yank.

It *was* a car. A small, round one. Bright yellow.

"What is that?" Bingo asked.

Al smiled. "'65 Volkswagen Beetle. I take it you've never seen one?"

"I've never even heard of one."

"Naw, you wouldn't. Seein' as how this is 2019, this car's fifty-four years old now. But back then, it was Olivia's pride and joy. We bought it used for her in '77 when she got her license. She'd just turned sixteen."

"Does it run?"

"Sure it does. I keep air in the tires, the battery charged and fluids changed. And every month or so I drive it down to the highway and back."

Bingo was admiring it when Al walked over and handed him something. *Car keys.* "It's yours, son. I want you to have it."

It took Bingo a moment to realize what Al was saying.

"What? No. No, I couldn't. No way. You need it."

"Not anymore. It's not servin' any real purpose here. Now it can. You never did tell me where you two are headed."

"The mountains," Bingo answered. "I just want to see some mountains."

"Well, for mountains you'll need to go to New Mexico—I'd say Red River or Taos. I personally prefer those in Colorado myself. There're a few near Trinidad and La Veta. And a big one east of Alamosa. But you want those at South Fork. I love that town. Not a fast food place or shoppin' mall one there. Just a mom and pop grocery/hardware store that has it all, a fillin' station and a handful of great hole-in-the-wall places to eat. Don't find many places like it these days. Especially surrounded by mountains. From there, the farther north you go, the bigger and higher the mountains get. And, they're all a *long* walk from here. You need this car. You have a license?"

"No sir. My dad didn't think I needed one."

"Do you know how to drive?"

"Yes sir. A friend of mine taught me with his car. My dad doesn't know."

"Can you drive a stick-shift?"

"Yes sir! His had a manual transmission."

"Then you're all set. No license or insurance, but if you take it easy and are careful, you should be all right. Oh, and one more thing." He walked around to the rear and opened the trunk. Instead of storage space, there sat an engine—a little bitty one. "Motor's back here. The jack, spare and gas tank are up front. Plus a little room to store things."

Bingo nodded and then looked over at me. If I could

talk, he'd know whatever he decides is fine with me, but if I have a vote, I sure prefer riding over walking. Especially in summer. So I was left with wagging my tail. He looked out through the barn door, thinking. The rain was coming down in sheets. Finally, he turned toward Al.

"How can I ever repay you?"

"By findin' whatever it is you're lookin' for. And never givin' up till you do. That's how."

Bingo hugged Al, crying. "Yes sir. I promise."

They shared a long embrace. Then Al pulled away and smiled. "All right then. Let's get this thing warmed up." He walked over and opened the driver's door. I jumped in and took my place in the passenger seat, noticing immediately that I could see over the dash. Cool. That deserved a bark. They laughed and Bingo threw his backpack into the back seat, climbed in, inserted the key, turned it, and the little car came to life. We sat there listening to it idle. Bingo rolled down his window and Al leaned in.

"Here's the title. Keep it in a safe place but not in the car. There's some money in the glove box there. Fifty or sixty dollars if I recall. Olivia had cashed some baby-sittin' checks and forgot it was in there. That was her. She'd even forget to tie her shoes sometimes. Always goin' ninety-to-nothin'."

"Al, I—"

"You take that money. You'll need it. You've got dog food to buy. And I recommend gettin' a sleepin' bag too. Save the motels for showers when you need 'em."

Bingo nodded without speaking.

"All right, then." He turned toward me. "John, it's been an honor. You take good care of this fella, you hear?"

I barked a loud yes and they both laughed. Al and Bingo then shook hands through the window.

"So long, son. The road is yours."

Bingo smiled, stepped on the clutch and shoved the shifter into gear with a long, loud, grinding noise. His face turned red.

"Don't you worry, son. Try as she may, my Olivia never could harm those gears. You won't either."

Bingo smiled again, gave it some gas, let out on the clutch and with a lurch we were off. As we drove away, he looked at Al through the rear view mirror. Our friend was standing out in the rain, waving. With joy in his heart and a tear in his eye. Same as Bingo.

CHAPTER 8

BINGO

An hour or so later we pulled into Tyler. Sure enough, about the first thing we saw was a Walmart. I found a buggy in the parking lot. I picked John up and stuffed him in the buggy, and we started inside. We got some stares, but no one said anything. John was obviously very pleased with being chauffeured around. He kept looking at me like, "Why are we not doing more of this?" He was so obvious that I laughed out loud. What a big goober! I bought some canned food, a toothbrush, a cheap sleeping bag, a small flashlight, a small umbrella, a big bag of Ol' Roy dog food, and a map. I knew I couldn't afford to waste gas by getting lost. I had never really been very far from home. Joel Bookman had never been the family outing or family vacation type, which suited us just fine. I could not think of very many things that sounded less appealing to me than spending several hours in a car with him. Then we hit the road again.

I have to admit that I was more than a little herky jerky with my starts and shifts. John, who was mostly content to lie quietly on the seat beside me, would occasionally raise an eyebrow and shoot me a look like, "Are you trying to kill us?" But soon I was getting a little better at not grinding the gears or trying to throw us through the windshield. We hit the interstate and headed west and north. Those were the only two directions I would allow us to go. I was determined we were never going back.

I tried the radio, but in all honesty the sound of an AM radio in a '65 Volkswagen can best be described as tinny. John covered his ears. So I turned it off and we cruised along with the windows down. Our mood was soaring. I had never been exposed to such kindness and generosity before like Al's. I wasn't even sure that those kind of people existed. I really struggled to try to come to grips with all of this, but John's attitude seemed to be, "Hey, we ain't walking. Don't look a gift horse in the mouth." So I decided that he was probably right, and we should just enjoy the moment.

The interstate was just what we needed. We could drive at a speed that didn't waste fuel, and there was another lane for everybody (and I mean everybody) else to go around us. I have to admit we got more than a few unfriendly remarks and gestures from people who thought we were going too slow. But we were too elated to even be the least bit bothered by all of that. I kept wondering why everybody was in such a big hurry. The speed limit sign said 75 mph, but most of the drivers ignored that like it didn't even exist.

We were making pretty good time, and before long we were getting close to Dallas. I started seeing these signs about a place called Buc-ee's in Terrell. Evidently, according to the signs, Buc-ee's had everything. So when we got there I pulled in. We needed gas anyway, and they must have had a hundred gas pumps. We went inside. Those signs weren't lying. They had more stuff than I had ever seen. And people were everywhere. And they had the cleanest restrooms I had ever seen. We wandered around for a while, and just like at Walmart we got some stares, but that's all. I bought some jerky for John and a big Icee for me and we were off again.

As we neared Dallas, it occurred to me Tyler was the biggest city I had ever been to. I couldn't imagine this many people wanting to live so close together. What were they thinking?

As luck would have it, my luck anyway, we arrived right about 5:00 p.m. A word to people from small towns: That is a mistake you never want to make. I thought there must have been a jillion cars on the road. And at least half of them either couldn't see me or could see me and didn't care, and seemed determined to run smooth over us. Traffic slowed to a crawl, which was just fine with John. He was no longer content to lay in the seat. He was sitting up, straining to take in everything he could. He kept looking over at me as if to say, "Are you seeing this? Are you believing this?" Neither of us had ever seen buildings that big or tall. Or so many cars hell bent on trying to get to the same place. I let out a small laugh and said, "Well, buddy, I hope neither of us has to go pee. Cause there ain't nowhere to go."

The map told us to stay on this interstate all the way through Dallas into Fort Worth. So we drove right through the middle of both cities at the worst possible time. To be honest with you, I couldn't tell where one place ended and another one began. It was just one giant blob of human-ity to me. Finally we hit US 287 and turned north trying to get out of Fort Worth. Half an hour later, we actually began to see some countryside and a little less traffic. I felt like we were lucky to escape with our lives. In all honesty, I had regretted that Icee for about the last half hour or so. We found a Burger King, and I borrowed the facilities and John borrowed the parking lot. We stretched our legs and tried to release the tension in our bodies.

It was getting close to dark by now, and I saw a sign that said, "Wichita Falls 90 Miles". I told John to just hang in there and we would try to make it there to spend the night. The stress of getting through all of that traffic, for me, and the excitement of it all, for John, had been so great that neither one of us even thought about being hungry. So we just drove into the night.

It wasn't long before we could see lightning flashes far in the distance. And the farther we drove, the closer and brighter they got. By the time we got to Wichita Falls, we could hear the thunder. My plan was to spend the night in a warm sleeping bag, but it sure looked like rain and John was looking at me pleadingly and whimpering. When John gives me a look like that, I always wilt. "OK, buddy. Let's find a cheap motel." It wasn't too long until we saw a motel sign and a marquee that said, "Cheapest Rates in Town". I pulled in. I went into the office and gave the guy twenty dollars and got a key. "No pets!" he growled at me as I walked out the door. "No problem," I said, and kept on walking. After all, John was no pet. I grabbed my backpack from the car, and we went inside. We were dog tired. Pardon the expression.

CHAPTER 9

BINGO

I woke up the next morning with John bouncing up and down on the bed and licking my face. "Come on, man," I said, trying to cover myself from a tongue assault. I lay there for a moment quite pleased with myself and my decision to get a motel for the night. It looked like the weather had a chance to get really bad, and I had heard all the stories and was pretty sure that outside in Wichita Falls all night during a bad storm was not really the best place to be. And while our room would never be confused with the Ritz, we were warm, dry, and safe. Plus I could now take a shower, a luxury that I vowed to take advantage of. I was feeling so good that I told John as soon as I got dressed we were going to find ourselves a good hot breakfast.

As I would soon learn, there is nothing more civilizing than being able to take a shower and brush your teeth. Going one day without a shower was maybe okay. Two days was definitely not, and three days was disgusting. I swore to myself that I would never do that.

I grabbed my backpack and threw open the door, eager to take on a new day. Life was good!

But, wait, *where was the car?* I had parked it here last

night, but it was nowhere to be seen. What could have happened? I looked around frantically. My heart was racing and I could feel myself starting to panic. John was looking as confused as I was.

Finally the realization began to set in that the car had been stolen. I guess, in my fatigue and desire to get inside before the storm hit, I had left the keys in the car. I was crushed. Al had entrusted me with something very dear to him, and I had lost it within twenty-four hours. Plus, our prospects were suddenly a lot dimmer. I tried to think. I still had the title Al had signed over stuffed safely in my backpack, but how could I call the cops? I had no driver's license and no insurance. Plus how often do the cops find stolen vehicles? In less than two days we had seen just about the best humanity had to offer and now the worst that humanity had to offer. I sat down on the curb and hung my head.

Once again, John came to the rescue. I felt his head push against my leg. He was wagging his tail. His hope and his enthusiasm were infectious. I rubbed his head and got up. "Well buddy, we started out on foot and I guess we are walking again. No matter what they throw at us, we are going to hang together and keep going."

CHAPTER 10

JOHN

I know it was a cheapie, but I thought our motel room was nice. It wasn't fancy but it was cozy. Following dinner and a quick walk around the premises to take care of business, I quickly claimed my side of the bed while Bingo flipped through the channels on the little TV. My TV watching days were extremely limited back home. Only on the rare occasion Joel was out of town, and then I had to stay off the couch for fear he'd find a single hair of mine. Nobody wanted to find out what would happen if that occurred. Bingo landed on *Hondo*, a great old John Wayne movie I happened to have seen before. I remembered it because Hondo's smart and loyal canine companion (Is there any other kind?) was simply called "Dog". Poor guy. Five minutes into it, Bingo was sound asleep. I stuck with it, and when it was over I closed my eyes for the night while some guy peddled pocket-sized rod and reels for avid fishermen.

With the car gone, our road adventure was quickly losing its luster. I'm pretty sure Bingo felt the same. By mid-morning it was hot; we were tired; and the road before us appeared to stretch on forever—which it kinda did. Then I remembered we hadn't really set out to see the sights. We were simply getting as far away from Joel Bookman as possible. Neither of us thought he would come looking for us. He was likely pissed about the ashtray to the head. (Bingo told me about that. And let me tell you, that'll make your tail wag.) But at the same time, he was probably happy we were gone and hoping we weren't coming back. He needn't worry.

But I know Bingo missed his mom. I did too. Lily was a sweetheart. But she was under Joel's control, and there was nothing anybody could do about it. Not once had she ever called the police or an ambulance when things got bad, and she should have. I wanted to think she'd be fine with us gone but knew different. With us out of the picture, Joel had only her to vent his frustrations and anger on. I hoped she'd be okay. For her sake. And Bingo's.

My line of thought was broken by the sound of a car slowing behind us. We moved over near the grass as it pulled up beside us—an old, white Impala with loud pipes and a stereo blaring. Inside were two twenty-somethings with shaved heads, wearing sleeveless T-shirts.

"The hell y'all doin'?" the passenger asked.

Bingo kept walking and didn't look up. The car stayed alongside us.

One of them turned down the music. "Hey, buddy! I asked you a question."

Bingo stopped and looked over. "We're just walking down the road. Minding our business."

"Y'all need a ride?"

"No thanks."

"You got any money?"

"No sir. If I did, we wouldn't be walking."

"You don't say."

The driver killed the engine, got out and walked around

the front of the car. I moved in front of Bingo and growled. He stopped.

"What kind of dog is that?"

"He's a mixed breed. I'm not sure."

I stared at the guy and growled even louder.

"I ain't afraid of that damn dog. I tell ya that right now. I can kick his ass *and* yours and take your damn money if I decide to."

"Well make up your mind," his passenger said. "I'm hungry."

"I really don't have any money," Bingo said again. "Just some dirty clothes, a little food and a toothbrush. That's all."

Heck, Bingo had *me* convinced. The guy didn't stand a chance. We watched him turn and get back in the driver's seat.

"No hard feelings? You know we were just funnin' with you, right?" the passenger asked.

"The hell you say! I'll whip their butts!" The driver opened his door again and started to get out. His buddy grabbed him by the shirt.

"Get your fat ass back in here, you doofus. I know you can. He knows it. And that funny-lookin' dog knows it. But right now we don't have the time. We have someplace to be, remember? And I'm still starvin'. Now let's go."

The driver spit out his window, started the car, gunned the engine, turned the music up loud, peeled out and sped away to the sound of Guns N' Roses singing *Welcome to the Jungle*. Bingo and I watched them go then looked at each other.

"Well, I think that went pretty well, don't you?" he asked, smiling. I barked and had a quick pee. "You were ready to tear into him, weren't you, buddy?"

Darn right I was.

"I'm not surprised. And I thank you. I guess we're looking out for each other."

Yep. We definitely were looking out for each other now. Bingo took a bottled water and paper cup from his backpack and poured some for me. I took a long drink. When I was finished, I looked up at him.

"That it? You done?"

Satisfied, I turned away. He drank from the bottle and replaced both. Then we headed on down the road toward Electra.

CHAPTER 11

JOHN

We didn't make it to Electra, but we got close. Just before dark set in, we climbed a fence bordering the road and headed out across a field. It might have been wheat at one time, or hay, but had been cleared and was covered with some sort of grass now. Once we were a ways from the road, Bingo stopped. His sleeping bag was long gone with the car. So was the Ol' Roy dog food. No hurt feelings here. Luckily, he still had his trusty backpack. He pulled out a can of Dinty Moore Beef Stew for us to share and looked at me.

"Just this one time until I can get some more dog food. You heard what Al said about you eating human food. I can't have you getting sick so don't expect this very often."

Fair enough.

Above us, the stars and moon were back. We were both pooped and sleep came quickly and easily. More dreams of chasing small animals. And a few large ones. And one of those grey, fast-moving things that roll up into a hard ball when caught. We'd come across one a few hours back. I want to say Bingo called it an Amarillo but that doesn't sound quite right. I'm not sure what it was.

The next day's walk was pretty uneventful. We made it to Electra around midday and true to his word, Bingo purchased a small bag of dog food at an Allsup's. It wasn't Ol' Roy and sure looked good in the picture. And it wasn't bad. To save money, Bingo was back to cheese crackers for his lunch. Rejuvenated after food and a short rest, we hit the road again. Shortly, we heard the familiar sound of a car slowing behind us. Thankfully, no loud pipes this time. Bingo stopped and looked. It was a man and woman in a silver Honda Accord. She rolled down her window.

"Are you okay?"

"Yes ma'am. We are."

"Can we give you a ride somewhere?"

To my great surprise, after a moment, Bingo answered, "Yes, ma'am. That would be great." We were hot and tired, but this wasn't like him. He'd only agreed to a ride with Al because it was pouring rain. I followed him to the car and into the back seat.

"This is very kind of you," he said.

The man and woman, middle-aged by my guess, looked at us.

"Headed anywhere particular?" the man asked.

"No sir. Just out for a walk."

"Where're you two from?"

"Center."

"Texas?"

"Yes sir."

"That's some walk, young man." He and the woman shared a look, then he put the car in gear and pulled away.

"You're not in any kind of trouble are you?" asked the woman.

"No ma'am. We're just adventurous."

That brought laughter from the two of them. Then,

"I'm Harry Winston. This is my wife Harriet." He turned and smiled at Bingo.

Bingo smiled. "Well, I'm Bingo and this here is John."

"You don't say. Well, it's a pleasure to meet the two of you. We are going as far as Clarendon if that helps any."

"Yes sir. That would be great. We're headed to the mountains."

"My goodness," the woman said. "New Mexico is a good ways off."

"Actually we're going to South Fork, Colorado."

"Oh, you'll love it there! We used to go every fall to see the leaves change. And it's such a wonderful little town."

"That's what we've heard."

"Any relatives there?"

"No ma'am."

"Well, there are a number of cabins available. And a lodge or two. No big chain motels though."

"That sounds great. Can't wait."

"And of course it'll be cooler there. Their summers aren't like ours."

"That's even better."

The remainder of the ride consisted of talk about the man and woman's kids and grandchildren. And the places they'd all been. No mention was made of Bingo's family. It was mid-afternoon when we reached Clarendon. They dropped us at a Dairy Queen. Following a shared vanilla shake (chocolate isn't good for dogs), we walked through town, passed a college on a hill and were soon leaving Clarendon and the Winstons behind.

We stayed the night in a small roadside park with a clean restroom and food and drink machines. Three hard, hot days and nights later we made it to Amarillo.

CHAPTER 12

BINGO

It was well past dark when we got to Amarillo. We were tired, dirty, straggly, and hungry. I kept thinking we looked much worse than Shaggy and Scooby even after they had just been scared by the monster. I just kept walking past convenience stores and fast food joints. John kept looking at me like, "Hello! Did I mention food?" But I just couldn't bring myself to do another gas station burrito or greasy fast food burger. Up ahead I kept seeing this bright glow like some kind of circus or something. The more we walked, the brighter the glow got. The bright lights were doing just what bright lights were supposed to do, luring me, pulling me toward them. When we got close, I saw that it was the Big Texan Steak House. Boy, I thought to myself, a big steak sounds wonderful right now. When we finally got to the parking lot, I just stood there. I knew there was no way we could afford the luxury of eating at some place like that. I felt so tired. For the first time, despair started to overtake me. Just then I noticed an awful odor. I looked at John and he had laid down and covered his nose with his paws. "What is that!?"

A big cattle truck had pulled into the almost empty

parking lot and stopped right beside us. The smell was disgusting. A cow started to pee out of the side of the truck. John and I jumped back to keep from getting splashed. The cab door opened, and a giant of a man crawled out. He looked like he could bench press a full-grown oak tree. His boots were covered with cow manure, and he had plenty more on his jeans. He smelled no better than the truck. He sized us up and down.

"Looks like you boys could use a good meal. Wanna have supper here with me?"

"No thanks, mister." I said haltingly. "This place is a little over our heads."

He grinned a big grin. "If I'm doin' the invitin', I'm doin' the buyin'. Won't cost you a thing. You sure you ain't interested? I won't ask again."

"Yes sir!' I said loudly.

He slapped my back, nearly knocking me down. "Let's go eat! My name is Cliff."

We introduced ourselves and he opened the door for us. We went inside and there stood the hostess. I thought she was the prettiest girl I had ever seen. I froze completely. Cliff looked at me and laughed. John head butted my leg. I think he was trying to tell me that if I was going to stare, at least close my mouth. Cliff told her we needed a table. She was hesitant. "I better get my manager," she said. Cliff nodded politely and very soon she was back with the manager.

The manager was a little guy, and he reeked of arrogance. "Is there a problem?" he asked. His voice was full of contempt.

"Nope, no problem," Cliff said agreeably, "We just want a table so we can eat."

"There is no way I can seat you," the manager sneered.

But Cliff did not bristle. "We know we look a little ragged," he said. And we won't be any trouble. Just sit us somewhere out of the way, and we won't let out a peep."

"The manager puffed out his chest. "I am not giving you a table!"

Cliff pulled out a big wad of cash. His voice got very quiet. "Our money is good and we will be big tippers. From the looks of your parking lot tonight, your staff could use the help."

"No," the manager insisted. "No way."

Cliff's whole persona changed. He became completely menacing, but he didn't raise his voice. He didn't have to. "Either you give us a table, or I'm gonna to start tearing this place apart. I can do a whole lot of damage before the cops get here."

The manager was a little uncertain now. "But I might lose my job if I let y'all in here." He was almost pleading.

"Yep, you might. But the way I see it, when I start throwing chairs through the windows and the local news finds out why I did it, I'm almost certain you'll lose your job then. So what's it gonna be?"

The manager decided that discretion was the better part of valor. "OK," he said. "But the dog stays outside."

"Not acceptable." Cliff said. "The dog comes too."

"But it is a health code violation!"

Cliff leaned it tight, just a few inches from the manager's face. "Do we look like the damn health department to you?"

The manager's self-importance shattered right before our eyes. "Right this way," he said, and he led us to a table about as far away from everything as he could find.

The hostess immediately came over. "I am so sorry," she said." We all hate that prick." John let out a high pitched bark and wagged his tail. She laughed.

It was true. Sad. But true. The dog had more game than I did.

Cliff ordered for us, and we had maybe the best tasting meal I have ever had in my whole life. I shared our story, and then we sat and laughed as Cliff told stories about all of his years of cowboyin'. Before the meal was over, the chef came out with a big sack. He'd made me a steak for the road, and he had a bunch of leftovers and bones for John.

When we couldn't eat another bite, we left. Cliff told us that we were welcome to tag along with him, but he was going east—the wrong way, so we said no. John and I both thanked him profusely and started the other way. Both our load and our mood seemed much lighter. And was about to get even lighter. You never know when something good might be just around the corner.

CHAPTER 13

JOHN

---

*T*here it was. Our yellow VW Beetle! We couldn't believe it. What were the chances? Cliff noticed our excitement and walked over.

"Well I'll be. That the one you were tellin' me about?"

"Sure is!" Bingo was trying the door but found it locked.

Then we heard, "Hey! *Get away from there!*"

We all turned and spotted a young man and woman
rushing our way. They didn't look much older than Bingo.
The guy squeezed in between Bingo and the car door.

"What the hell you think you're doin'?"

"This is our car," Bingo said. "It belongs to John and me."

"The hell it does."

Bingo looked through the window. "So does that sleeping bag and that dog food in the back seat."

Can't say I was thrilled to get the Ol' Roy back, but it was
a small price to pay to keep from having to walk to Colorado.

"Bullshit. Get lost."

Cliff had heard enough. He walked over. The woman's
eyes grew big.

"'Scuse me, what's your name, son?"

"Who's askin'?"

Cliff smiled. "The guy who's gonna rip your legs off and tie 'em to this car." He turned and looked at Bingo. "Ever had any curb feelers, Bingo?"

"No sir."

"Naw you wouldn't. You're too young." He turned back to the car thief. "And when I'm done with you, I'm gonna make a hood ornament out of your friend there."

Her eyes grew really big. She looked over at her boy-friend. "Let's go, sweetie."

You could see the wheels turning in the guy's head. It didn't take long for them to mesh and come up with the correct answer.

"Yeah. Whatever." And the two of them started to walk away.

"Hold on, pardner," Cliff called out.

They stopped and turned.

"The keys."

Car thief guy's first thought was to throw them at Cliff. His second, and a much more sensible one, was to walk over and hand them to Bingo. Which he did.

"Satisfied?"

"Y'all have a good evenin'. What's left of it," Cliff answered.

We watched them leave, and Bingo turned to our friend.

"Thank you, Cliff. Again. First supper, now this. I don't know what to say."

"Nothin' to say. Now climb in. I wanna get a good look at the two of you in this thing."

We did as instructed.

Cliff smiled. "Yep. Just as I thought. This car was just made for you guys. You look great in it." He stuck his big hand through the window, and he and Bingo shook. "So long, fellas. Take care of yourselves."

"We will. I promise. Thanks again for everything."

The big man smiled as Bingo started the engine and pulled away. This driving away and leaving friends behind was becoming a habit. After a brief stop for gas, we were once again on the open road. In our yellow car.

CHAPTER 14

BINGO

I pulled out the map. It seemed to me that the best way to go was toward Dumas. So we shifted our direction back to the north. We had been going west or northwest for a week. Now it was time to head due north. I could not believe our stroke of good fortune. What were the odds of getting our car back? The great guilt I felt about how I had let Al down had been lifted away. I looked down at John. He didn't seem troubled by any of this at all. He was tired, his belly was full, and he wasn't having to walk. He was sound asleep. I guess the big meal and the roller coaster events of the past few hours were starting to catch up with me too. I knew I had to find a place to stop pretty soon. We found a nice roadside park on the northern outskirts of Amarillo, and I pulled in for the night. I was taking no chances. We were sleeping in the car.

The morning dawned bright and clear. There was just a hint of coolness in the air, but I knew it wouldn't last long. We both got out. Nature was calling us both pretty loudly. We needed to stretch anyway. Fortunately, our breakfast had been prepared for us the night before. Maybe my steak wasn't fresh and hot, but it sure beat a package of cheese crackers. And John was mighty grateful for the leftovers the cook had set aside for him. We had full bellies, and we washed it all down with some good gulps of water and it was time to go.

I had never seen anything like the panhandle of Texas. It was stark and huge and desolate. There were no landmarks. The emptiness and the loneliness and the vastness seemed to affect me deep inside. I had heard so many people say that the panhandle was ugly and boring. I did not share that feeling, but I did feel something.

We headed north for a while, and then it was time to turn back to the northwest.

We were so thrilled to be riding that we took our time, stopped quite often and just generally enjoyed the chance to not be hoofing it. No matter how much we tarried and messed around, we were still making so much better time than walking. Pretty soon we saw a sign that said, "Welcome to New Mexico". It was the first time I had ever been outside the boundaries of Texas. The terrain began to change, and everything started to get a little more hilly. We had gotten so used to flatness that even a small rise seemed towering to us.

It was around 2:00 in the afternoon, when we got to Clayton. I saw a big, rusty old sign that said, "Welcome to Clayton, New Mexico. Home of Charmayne James—World Champion Barrel Racer." What is a barrel racer? I wondered. Does someone stand on barrels and roll them with their feet? Or do they just give the barrel a big push and see which one gets down the hill the fastest? Whatever it was, I figured Charmayne James must have been pretty dang good at it.

We were starting to get a little hungry. John was giving me that look. We saw a Dairy Queen up ahead. Dinner last night had cost us nothing and breakfast had been free, too, so I reckoned it would be okay if we maybe had a burger or something. We parked and went in. I locked the doors and clutched the key tightly. There was no one else in the place. Just then a pretty young girl in a Dairy Queen uniform came out and walked over to our booth. She had jet black hair and dark eyes the size of saucers, and she smiled the sweetest smile I think I had ever seen. She was small and petite, and her DQ uniform fit her good. It fit her real good.

"Your dog can't come in here," she said sweetly. I asked if it would be okay if John just hid under the table. She looked around at the empty restaurant and decided nobody was going to get hurt. She nodded her head. "What would you like to eat?"

"I want a burger and fries and a big Coke," I said.

"And for him?"

"Give him some chicken strips. John's always had a fondness for fowl."

She soon brought our food. She said it was time for her lunch break and asked would we mind if she sat down and talked to us for a minute. I blushed and stammered a little bit and finally managed to get out the word *sure*.

She slid in the booth beside me. I suddenly had a hard time swallowing my food.

"Where y'all from?" she asked. "We don't get that many strangers through here."

For some reason my shyness deserted me, and I began to tell her the whole story from my abusive dad to kind, old Al and a stolen car and everything that had happened along the way. As she listened her eyes got bigger and bigger (I didn't think that would be possible), and a couple of times I thought I saw a tear. She gently laid her hand on mine. No girl had ever touched me like that before. If I am being honest, I would have to say I rather enjoyed it.

With all the talking and storytelling, we had soon finished our meal. "I guess we better be going ," I said. She glanced at her watch.

"I have just enough time left on my lunch to walk you outside." She smiled that sweet smile again.

We walked out to the car. "What a cool car!" She touched my hand again. Then she leaned in close and kissed me. I wish I could say that I was very cool and confident about this. I wish I could say that. Actually my knees were shaking. Girls had never shown any interest in me. I think they mistook shyness for weirdness. Then she did it again. And then I think I might've even kissed her. I'm not sure.

She looked at her watch. She leaned in, gave me one last long kiss and ran back into the restaurant. I stood there for several seconds and then climbed in the car.

I started the engine and suddenly realized that I hadn't put John in the car! I got out laughing and said, 'What's a matter, boy? Did you think I was gonna leave you? I would never leave you!" John just kept looking at me like he wasn't so sure. He jumped in and we took off. I drove quite a ways, smiling and not saying a word. Finally, John gave me a high pitched shrill bark. He was probably trying to tell me, "Get a grip, man."

But it did no good. I could not even begin to get a grip. It occurred to me that I hadn't had a shower in days. Oh, God! But she didn't seem to mind. Nothing like that had ever happened to me before. Stupid, I thought to myself. Why didn't I ask her name? I got the feeling that this would've been a game-changer—that I would never be the same again. Nothing and no one would ever come between me and John, but for the first time I really began to think about other possibilities in my life.

Very quickly my attention was captured by the hills. They were getting a lot taller. I told myself that I needed to call my mom and let her know we were okay. But the truth is we were more than okay. Just a very short time ago, my whole world consisted of dread, and fear, and hesitation. I could never have imagined what we would go through to get where we were right now. But, hey, we were still ticking. I was sure that some hard times might still lay ahead, but we had survived some hard times already. Maybe life did not have to always be terrible. Maybe, just maybe, we had what it takes. Maybe we might have a chance to amount to something after all.

CHAPTER 15

JOHN

I was fine with the whole kissing thing once I realized the girl's intentions were good. And I'm happy for Bingo. Other than his own mom, I don't think he's ever been kissed before. Certainly not on the mouth like that, bless his heart.

We headed on down the road leaving the girl and the experience behind. In a little while we passed through the tiny town of Des Moines and shortly after that, Capulin. Just outside of town we came upon a sign that read, "Capulin Volcano National Monument 7 Miles." Bingo turned off in that direction and looked over at me.

"I've read about this!" he said. "A volcano! In New Mexico! Can you believe it? But don't worry. It's not active. We gotta have a look at this."

I wasn't sure exactly what a volcano was. In the distance was a small mountain (or large hill), sitting in the open all by itself. That must be it. And it was. Five minutes later we were on the small paved road circling it on our way to the top. A few short minutes later, we reached the summit. There we found a paved parking lot, a plaque and some observation points. And the best thing was we had the place to ourselves. Not a soul around. We climbed out, and I peed while Bingo checked out the plaque.

"This thing's 60,000 years old! And get this, every spring all the trees and bushes are covered with thousands and thousands of ladybugs. Ain't that something?"

I knew what a ladybug was and was quite fond of them really. Not for eating, mind you, just for observing.

Bingo finished reading and stared into the distance. The view was quite spectacular in every direction. It seemed we could see forever. Bingo grew quiet. Vastness can certainly make one feel tiny, and I'm guessing that's what he was feeling. Or maybe he was thinking about the girl. I don't know. Finally, he turned and said, "Guess that's it, buddy. We've seen all there is to see here. Let's get going." I followed him to the car still unsure exactly what a volcano was, and we headed back down.

Happiness is a strange bird, that's for sure. For me, it just means Bingo and I are together. Throw in some food and water and everything's wonderful. It's more complicated for people. It's not your fault. That's just the way it is. Once we were back on the main highway, Bingo reached over and turned on the radio. A quick search revealed he had two stations to choose from. A distant one wracked with static and what sounded like Mexican music and a slightly stronger station playing Willie Nelson. He opted for Willie and turned it up.

A quick search of my own revealed there was nary a deer, rabbit or even a bird within viewing distance so my mind drifted to equally important matters, and I quickly reached the conclusion that as much as I'd like to be able to walk upright or sit and play a piano, being a dog does have its perks. For instance, most of us can run pretty fast and jump pretty well. And, of course, we have an outstanding sense of sight and smell. I can spot a squirrel three blocks away. We can eat darn nearly anything (dead or alive) without stomach upset and don't mind getting stinky. In fact, I think I'd enjoy a good roll in some fresh cow poop or horse poop should we come across any. Nor do we care about having bad breath. We also can go days, weeks, even months without a haircut and be perfectly satisfied. Same goes for baths. And if we behave in a halfway decent manner, complete strangers are quick to talk sweet to us and want to pet us. All good things. But, there is a flip side. Things we don't like. And it's a fairly long list. Let's see . . . Haircuts, baths, chains, leashes, fleas, ticks, sirens, thunder, wheels of any kind, rashes, going to the vet, having our picture taken, and worst of all—not nearly enough years on this earth. Why that is I'm not sure. We are loyal; our love is unconditional; and we don't pollute or abuse the planet in any form or fashion. We should be allowed to hang around longer. Don't you think?

Having said all that, we dogs each have our own distinct personality. Many can be described as finicky, cranky, impatient, stubborn or independent. I've tried hard not to be any of these. Bingo has always had more than his share of problems to deal with. He doesn't need any more, and I've tried my best not to give him any.

So, if I had my druthers, I prefer being a member of the canine family. Except for that short life span business. That makes about as much sense to us dogs as a game of fetch.

CHAPTER 16

JOHN

The sign ahead read, "Raton 28 Miles". We arrived half an hour later around 4:00 p.m. Bingo looked over.

"No sleeping bag or back seat for us tonight, boy. Tonight it's a hot shower and a comfy bed. We are overdue. *And*, we are upgrading this time around. Tonight our motel will have a name we've heard of." And it did. Best Western.

Bingo checked us both in (Pets Allowed!) and luckily was able to park directly in front of our room. That way we could keep an eye on the car and an ear out for any suspicious sounds. Following my potty break, Bingo gathered up our stuff (all of it this time), and we went inside. The room was really nice and smelled great. I thought I detected the faint aroma of a previous canine visitor but wasn't sure. It definitely wasn't feline. Bingo hit the shower and a few minutes later came what I'd been dreading, but expecting.

"John! Come! Your turn!"

Dang.

I took my time getting there. He opened the shower door.

"Come on, boy. It's not that bad."

Easy for you to say. I reluctantly stepped in, the door was closed behind me and I was greeted by the warm pelting water. Actually, it felt pretty good. The soaping and scrubbing, not so much. I was then rinsed clean. As soon as Bingo opened the door, I jumped out, shook off, and took off running like a wild man. I ran about the room, back and forth at breakneck speed, occasionally jumping up on the bed and then back down. This went on for a few minutes while Bingo dried himself off and laughed.

"I don't know why you always do that," he chuckled.

Truth is, I didn't either. It was like I was momentarily possessed. Anyway, the feeling finally subsided and I hopped up on the bed to stay. After our big breakfasts and then burgers and chicken strips at 2:00, Bingo said he wasn't hungry. Me, I'm *always* hungry. He turned on the large flat screen TV, and after a quick run through the channels Bingo remembered a laundry visit was called for. What few clothes he'd brought were in dire straits, in both look and smell. And we needed gas, so he grabbed the keys and we left.

A mile down the main drag we stopped at a Family Dollar store. Not a Walmart, but it would definitely suffice. He parked and said, "You stay here and guard the car, buddy. I'll just be a minute. I gladly did as I was told. No potential thieves surfaced and in no time he was back, wearing a new pair of jeans, a new bright blue T-shirt and a new pair of sneakers. His old stuff was in the sack along with some additional new underwear and socks. Bingo was set. We quickly found a coin-operated laundry and spent the next hour washing and drying clothes. I got a few looks from customers wondering what a dog was doing inside, but Bingo had seen no reason for me to stay in the car. We had a clear view of it right out the big plate glass window. He spent part of the time studying his map.

"We'll be in South Fork tomorrow. I'm thinking we might

stay there for a while. We'll have to sleep outdoors some-where because of our money situation, but the weather's still nice, and if it rains we have the car. That'll give us time to rest up and decide what we're gonna do next. How's that sound?"

It sounded fine to me. I was pretty sure ol' Joel wasn't on our trail but, to tell you the truth, I kinda wished he was. I don't think Bingo would object if I tore into to him now. Joel's terms didn't matter anymore. This was *our* world. And if we teamed up, we'd get the best of him I'm sure. And he'd finally get what he deserved. Boy, would I like that. I was just envisioning clamping down on Joel's private parts when Bingo finished gathering his clothes and said, "Let's go."

Two blocks down the road he pulled into a Conoco sta-tion. He inserted the nozzle and leaned against the car as the gas pumped. I was checking things out through my open window when the fella across from us finished up and walked over. He looked to be about forty and was dressed in pressed khakis and a nice golf shirt. He looked at our plates.

"Texas, huh?"

Bingo looked up from his daydream. "Yes sir."

"Whereabouts in Texas?"

"Out east. Near Tyler."

"No kidding. I'm from Nacogdoches. But I live in Denver these days."

"Cool."

"The name's Luke. Yours?"

"John." I didn't know if Bingo was being cautious or just didn't feel like getting into whole 'I'm Bingo and my dog's name is John thing.' I don't blame him.

I noticed the man was eyeing the car.

"That a '65 or '66?"

"1965."

"You don't say. Well, it's a beauty. Still run good?"

"Yes sir. Like a top."

The man smiled. "Don't guess you'd sell it, would you? I'd pay top price. I have a son who'd love it."

"No sir. I couldn't do that."

"I understand." He looked over at me. "What kind of dog is that?"

"Not sure. He's a mixed breed."

"Don't reckon you'd sell *him*, would you? My daughter would love him."

Bingo smiled. "No sir. Can't do that either. I need 'em both."

"Fair enough. Well, it was nice meeting you, John. You take care."

"Thank you. You too."

The man named Luke left, and Bingo looked in at me and smiled.

"There are some mighty strange people in this world."

I'd learned that a long time ago. He finished up, went inside to pay and returned with a ham and cheese sandwich and a Coke. I knew what that meant. Dog food for me back at the motel. There was still some left in the bag. When we got back, we were happy to see the parking spot in front of our room was still available. Bingo parked and made double sure the car was locked. Once inside, he turned on the TV, poured me some dog food and water and pulled out his sandwich and Coke. We watched the local news and weather as we ate. Twenty minutes later, we both fell asleep just as a woman was winning an all-expense-paid trip to Bermuda on Wheel of Fortune.

CHAPTER 17

BINGO

Who needs an alarm clock? I woke up once again with John licking my face. John was my one true companion, but I had just about decided that I preferred being kissed by a girl to being licked by a dog. Speaking of being kissed by a girl, I spent the whole night dreaming about a waitress. I have never done that before.

Since we had gotten all cleaned up the night before, it didn't take us very long to get going. I looked out the window to check on the car at least three times before we were out the door. John had business to take care of and for some reason was in no hurry. I thought there must have been a lot of interesting smells to check out. Raton, New Mexico, was kinda pretty. It didn't look anything like East Texas. Judging from John, I guess the odors didn't smell like East Texas either.

Since we hit Amarillo, things had been really going our way, but I was a little concerned. The money was getting a little tight. We were really going to have to be careful. Trinidad, Colorado—yes, Colorado—was just up ahead. I figured I could get some kind of crackers or something and a Coke because we were going to have to start being more frugal. Sure enough, there was a 7-Eleven there and I pulled in. I ran inside, grabbed a few things and then came back out and let John do a little more investigating. He loved to investigate.

I was watching John when a big, burly man walked up. He had broad shoulders and forearms that made him look like Popeye. He wore blue coveralls that had "Pearson Surveys" written in red over his heart and work boots that were very muddy. "Is that your Beetle?"

"Yes sir"

"Cool car," he said. That seems to be a consensus, I thought to myself. He eyed me up and down. "You just passin' through?"

"Yes sir," I said again.

"Are you in a hurry to get where you're goin'?"

"No sir."

He stuck out his hand. "My name's Paul Pearson."

I shook his hand. "We are John and Bingo."

"Hi, John." He pumped my hand up and down. I tried not to wince at his grip.

"No. I am Bingo. John is the dog."

He gave us a quizzical look and shrugged his shoulders. "You gotta last name, Bingo?"

"No. Just Bingo."

He shrugged his shoulders again and grinned. "OK. I wonder if you might be interested in helping me out a little bit? One of my guys just became a new daddy and is gonna take a few days off. That's gonna leave me a little short-handed. I could use an extra hand for a few days if you are interested. It'll mainly just be washing equipment and a little liftin' and movin' but nothing you can't handle. And you can even stay at my shop. I got showers and a cot. Pay is twelve bucks an hour." He eyed me up and down again.

"No," he said, "make that thirteen. Interested?"

"Yes sir!" He stuck out his hand again. This time I was the one doing the pumping.

"Follow me," he said, and he jumped into a big four-wheel drive pickup that looked like it might be new but was so muddy I couldn't really tell.

We followed him to his shop. There were all kinds of equipment there. I recognized the trucks as oil field trucks much like the ones in East Texas. There were cranes and trailers and all sorts of big pieces of pipe-looking things in racks. There were four or five guys in the shop when we walked in. They all had on the blue coveralls that also said "Pearson Surveys." One of the men grinned. "Whatcha got here, Paul?"

Paul grinned right back. "I just hired me a new vice-president. Vice President of Pressure Washing. You guys better do what he says." For some reason they all thought that was really funny.

He showed me around a little bit and pointed out where the cots were and the bathroom and showers. There was also a fridge and washer and dryer. Then he took me out back to this big trailer-mounted pressure washer. He showed me how to fill up the tank with water and the soap dispenser with soap, and then he fired it up. He told me he would be right back and then pulled around in his pickup and winked at me. "Your first assignment, Mr. Vice President, is to get this damn truck clean. And I mean clean. Holler when you're done."

I went to work. One minute later, I thought to myself: so much for clean hair and clean clothes. Water and mud were going everywhere, and I seemed to be attracting most of the residue. I was quickly sopping wet and covered in grime. But it wasn't anything I couldn't do as long as I wasn't concerned about getting wet and dirty. There were trucks to clean and pickups to clean and lots of those pipe-looking things to clean, and I was busy all day except for a couple of breaks that the guys made sure I took and a thirty minute lunch. One of the guys went to town to get burgers, and he got me one too. He even got a junior burger for John. John then decided that these guys were gonna be friends for life.

I worked until sundown, and then Paul told me it was time to knock off for the night. "Get some rest," he said, "cause mornin' will come early. But wash those clothes. And take a damn shower!" He was laughing. I was black from head to toe.

So this was my life for the next three days, sunup to sundown. Wet and dirty and tired. But they all treated me fair. They poked a little fun, but they poked a little fun at each other too and it was all in good humor. At 5:00 p.m. on the third day, Paul walked out the back door and hollered at me. I turned off the pressure washer and walked over to him. He handed me $300 in cash. "Here you go, son. An honest three days' pay for an honest three day's work. Take off early, get cleaned up, and go into town and blow off a little steam. You can stay here again tonight. Here's a key. It will get you in the gate and the back door."

CHAPTER 18

BINGO

I got cleaned up and John and I headed to town for dinner. It felt great to have extra money again. We quickly spotted a drive-in burger stand and pulled in. There were a bunch of kids about my age there, and they were all out of their cars and hanging out. I didn't think too much about it. I was busy studying the menu, trying to figure out what to order for John and me.

A very pretty girl walked over. She was maybe even prettier than the hostess in Amarillo and the waitress in Clayton. The way she carried herself made me think that she was very aware of how pretty she was. She leaned into my rolled down window.

"What a cool car," she said, smiling.

I was starting to notice a theme here. I wanted to say, "I get that a lot." But all I said was, "Thank you."

She looked at John. "What a sweet puppy!"

I looked at John. He wasn't buying it. There was no tail wagging, no eagerness to please that is always so obvious in a dog's body language. He was looking at her like, "I ain't no puppy, lady."

She leaned in even closer and asked me things like

where we were from and where we were going. She was obviously flirting with me. I was obviously enjoying it. John was not so thrilled. He even gave me a warning small growl or two. But I was becoming too full of myself to pay John any mind. She kept talking and smiling and playing with her hair and touching my arm. I was quickly under her spell and she knew it. She was enjoying it.

At that moment, another car pulled up and four boys wearing letter jackets got out. They immediately came over to my car. "Hey," the driver and the biggest one of the bunch said. "What the hell do you think you are doing? That's my girlfriend you're talking to."

'We were just sitting here," I replied. "She came over to us."

"So now you're accusing her of coming on to you? A scrawny homely little wimp like you? Get your skinny ass out of that car!"

"I am not looking for trouble."

"Too bad," letter jacket guy said, opening my door and reaching in to grab me. "You've already found it!"

He grabbed me by the shirt and pulled me out of the car. I spilled out onto the concrete. I started to get up, and he hit me on the mouth. Blood spurted from my split lip. I had been hit in the face many times before, so this was something I was not unaccustomed to. He stood there smiling, thinking that I would just run away. But I swung with all my might and returned the favor. Blood began to trickle from his nose. Two of his buddies jumped on me, and each one grabbed an arm. They stood me up in front of him. I was helpless. His first punch was to my ribs, knocking the breath out of me. Then he hit me in the face a few times and then once more hard right in the stomach. He might have thought he was badass, but Joel Bookman had hit me a lot harder many times before, and he didn't need any help. I watched as the fourth member of his little party took a baseball bat and rammed the end of it into both of the headlights on the VW. John was going crazy barking and snarling inside the car, and the guy was about to swing the bat into the passenger window when another car pulled in next to us. The two guys holding me let go. I fell to the ground. The other guy put the bat down and walked away.

I got back in the car and looked at John. "Are you okay, buddy?" He continued to bark. I started the car and we left. As we drove away, I looked back at the pretty girl. She had one arm around letter jacket guy's arm and was laughing and waving. I am such an idiot, I thought to myself. I had totally been played.

We made it back to Paul's shop and managed to get the gate opened and closed and went inside. Thankfully no one was there. I stumbled to the cot and passed out.

Paul and his guys began to arrive the next morning. They took one look at me and wanted to know what happened and were plenty upset about it. "Looks like they did a little job on the Volkswagen too."

Paul said, "Don't you worry about a thing. You just stay here today, rest and recuperate. The boys and I will get the headlights replaced on your car. You just heal up."

That day was pretty much a blur. I do know that John was right there at my side all day. I guess one of the guys must have called his wife and told her what happened because a lady came out to the shop right before noon with a bunch of fried chicken, mashed potatoes and gravy, and a big apple pie. I couldn't take too big a bite because if I opened my mouth very far, my lip would crack open and start bleeding again. But I did manage to eat. Mostly I just slept.

The next morning I slept right through everybody

coming in. When I finally woke up, it was nearly 10:30. The guys were just finishing changing the headlights on the car. Evidently no one in Trinidad, Colorado, kept headlights for a '65 Beetle in stock. Paul had had them FedExed in overnight.

I took a shower. The hot water helped a lot. I felt a lot better. When you are sixteen, I guess you heal up pretty quick. I was still sore, but then I had been there before. I loaded all our stuff up in the car. The guys presented me with a card. Inside was a hundred dollars, a collection they had taken up among themselves. My voice was about to break, but I told them all how much I appreciated everything they had done for me. "I will never be able to repay you," I said.

"Sure you will," Paul replied. "Just always try to do the right thing, to be a good man. That is the only way any of us can ever repay the rest of us."

I shook each of their hands, loaded John and myself into the car and hit the road again. I was trying not to cry.

CHAPTER 19

JOHN

The drive from Trinidad to South Fork was uneventful. And after the past twenty-four hours, uneventful was much welcomed. Since we hadn't eaten breakfast, we stopped in Walsenburg around 11:30 for lunch. Bingo found a small KFC and went through the drive-thru and loaded us up on chicken and fries and a Coke for him and a water for me. The guy in the window eyed Bingo's battered face but said nothing. Bingo then pulled around to the side and parked and rolled down the windows. A cool breeze drifted through the car. We sat there enjoying the food and the weather. When we were done, only the bag and drink cups remained. All evidence of the feast were gone. Bingo went in for a quick potty break and took me for mine when he returned. My stomach full and bladder empty, I settled in for a nap while Bingo pulled away. He woke me about an hour later.

"Looky there, boy. A *big* mountain!"

I looked and there it was. Sitting all by itself. We had seen a few a ways back, but nothing like this.

"That's Mount Blanca. Fourth-highest peak in Colorado."

It was pretty impressive. Despite it still being summer,

---

it appeared to be snow-covered. Before long, it was behind us and we were soon entering Alamosa. It was a fairly large town and took a while to navigate through because of construction. Once we left the city limits, Bingo looked at me.

"If I didn't know better, I'd say we were back in the Texas Panhandle. South Fork is only about fifty miles from here. I hope those mountains Al talked about show up pretty soon. I'm starting to get worried we're headed for the wrong South Fork."

I took a worried look over the dash and thought I could see what appeared to be mountains in the distance in the direction we were headed, but wasn't sure. They looked a million miles away. I hoped not. I looked over at Bingo. He definitely was concerned.

We needn't have been. In just under an hour, after passing through the quaint villages of Monte Vista and Del Norte, we were on the outskirts of South Fork, Colorado. Population: 349. Surrounded by tall mountains on three sides, we passed several realty businesses, a couple of lodges with small cabins for rent, a vet clinic, some gift shops and then spotted the Rainbow Grocery—the combo grocery/hardware store Al spoke of. And nearby, a small convenience store with gas pumps. Bingo parked in front of the Rainbow Grocery and headed in. He soon returned with some packaged and canned food and water.

"What a cool place!" he said, climbing in. "On the bottom floor are groceries, sporting goods for fishing and hunting, movies for rent and magazines, and upstairs is anything a guy would ever need in the way of plumbing, electrical or mechanical repairs. *And* clothes and shoes and boots of all kinds. *And* toys. It's crazy. Who needs a mall?"

Bingo's excitement reflected his good mood. The beating from the night before had been forgotten. He smiled, backed out and drove away.

One thing we'd noticed upon entering Colorado was there were campgrounds everywhere. And I mean everywhere. After a quick jaunt through the little town, we chose a small, deserted campsite just west of South Fork right on the Rio Grande River. On the radio, a station in Alamosa said it was 82 degrees with an expected low of 60 for the night. We parked, locked the car and explored up and down the bank for a while. Sometime around 5:00, Bingo set dinner out on our campsite's little picnic table. Dog food for me and Vienna sausages and crackers for him. When we were done, we went down to the bank and sat watching the cool water rush past. I think Bingo found it peaceful and soothing. I know he was deep in thought. We sat there nearly an hour in silence. Finally, with the sun low in the sky, he stood and I led the way back to our campsite. At sunset he pulled out his sleeping bag and laid it beside the car. He then stretched out on it with me at his side. It was early for bedtime, but I knew he was exhausted and sore and in need of another good night's sleep. Fifteen minutes later after staring at the stars and listening to the river, we were both sound asleep. Somewhere around midnight my peaceful dream of chasing field larks through a meadow was suddenly interrupted. By smell and sound. I opened my eyes to find the biggest cat I'd ever seen standing just feet away. He looked to be twice my size. Didn't matter. Whatever he had in mind wasn't going to play out. Especially if it involved Bingo.

I went at him.

CHAPTER 20

JOHN

I remember hearing his screeching and howling and Bingo's yelling above my barks. I got a few good bites in, but he was strong and quick and overpowering. We were rolling in the grass when he suddenly turned and ran. I remember trying unsuccessfully to stand and Bingo kneeling over me crying. I could feel him lifting me and placing me in the VW's passenger seat. Everything seemed to be moving in slow motion. It felt like a dream. He ran around, jumped in and we sped away.

"You're gonna be all right, boy. Just don't move. You're gonna be fine." He was racing toward town, wiping away tears, trying to see the road. My neck, back and legs felt like they were on fire. Before long he wheeled to a stop and he jumped out. I could hear him banging on a door and yelling.

"Hello? Hello! Please! Open up! We need help!" He did this for a minute or so then returned. "There's no one here, John. It's late. They're not open. I don't know what I was thinking. The car was still running, its headlights lighting the front of the small building. Bingo hit the steering wheel hard with his fists.

"Help us," he pleaded. *"PLEASE!* John's a good dog. *The*

best. He's never hurt anyone. All he's done is taken care of me. And I *can't* lose him. Not now." He sighed, leaned his head against the steering wheel and then softly cried, "I can't do this alone. Don't you understand? I can't go on without him."

A vehicle pulled in next to us. A red pickup. The driver rolled down his passenger window. Bingo jumped out.

"There a problem, son?" the driver asked.

"Yes sir! My dog's hurt bad. He needs help!"

"I'll call Doc Worley. He don't live far from here. Just sit tight."

"You hear that, boy? Help's coming. Hang on."

I sure hoped so. I was hurting pretty bad and dizzy. I closed my eyes. The next thing I remember is waking up on a table inside. The man from the pickup and another man, younger, with short hair and a beard were standing over me. So was Bingo.

"That should do it. No major damage. Nothing life-threatening anyway. It'll take a while for the wounds to heal. Some are pretty deep. There is some muscle damage. He'll need to stay here a couple of days but should be back on his feet by Monday."

"You hear that, John? You're gonna be okay." The crying was back. "Thank you Doc. Thank you so much. And you, sir. Thank you for stopping and helping us. You saved his life."

"I don't know about that."

"He's right, Ed. If you hadn't called me when you did, the dog most likely would have bled to death."

"Well, I'm just glad I happened by when I did. Someone was lookin' out for you, son. That's all I can say. Whatta you think it was, Doc? Bobcat?"

"That'd be my guess. A pretty big one from the looks of those bites. He looked at Bingo. "Did you see it?"

"No sir. I was asleep when the fight started. It was over before I could get my flashlight. You don't think he'll come back, do you?"

"No. I doubt it. It appears your dog got in some good shots of his own judging from what I found in his paws and teeth. I doubt you'll see that cat back anytime soon."

"That's a brave dog you got there, fella," the man called Ed said.

"I know he is. Always has been."

"Well, I best get goin'. So long, Doc. See you at the coffee shop Saturday?"

"I'll be there."

"Bye, son."

Bingo hugged him and watched through the widow as the man climbed in his pickup and left. He turned his attention back to the vet.

"So I can come get him day after tomorrow?"

"I think so. I'd just like to keep an eye on him until then. To be safe."

Bingo leaned close. "I'm leaving, buddy. You're gonna stay here and rest and get a couple of nights' sleep. Then I'll be back for you. You know I'll be back."

I knew he would. That's one thing about us dogs; people can look each other straight in the eye and lie and get away with it. But don't try that with us. One look into your eyes, and we know. Trust me. Bingo had never lied to me and wasn't about to start.

Through my haze I watched him hug the vet and leave. I remember the doctor carrying me to the back and carefully placing me in a small cage atop a blanket. I thought I heard other dogs in the room but wasn't sure. Then the world went black.

CHAPTER 21

BINGO

As I drove back to the campsite, my thoughts were racing and I was a jumble of emotions. I was mad at the bobcat for going after John. I was mad at John for going after the bobcat. I was overwhelmingly relieved that John was going to be okay. But I was also perplexed about praying so earnestly and some guy in a pickup showing up right then. That had to be some kind of a miracle. And I couldn't even begin to understand it, but while I was praying so hard, I felt some kind of connection. As if I knew someone was listening. More than just listening, responding.

I made it back to the campsite very late. I was exhausted. Taking no chances with the bobcat, I decided to sleep in the car. I kept looking up at the stars through the windshield, wondering what was out there. But very quickly, the adrenaline started to wear off and I drifted into a deep sleep. I guess the body can tell when rest is desperately needed.

I woke up later than usual the next morning. The sun was well clear of the eastern horizon. I went down to the river and splashed my face. The water was cold and I was instantly awake. I looked around. It was unbelievably beautiful here. I walked back to the car and slumped down with my back against the door, trying to take stock of everything that had happened.

The first thing I decided was that we were going to be here for a while. No travel until John was completely healed up and had his strength back. I knew that if I picked him up tomorrow and headed on down the road, he would not say a word. But I was determined not to do that to him. Everything was going to be about him for the next few days.

I drifted back to the day I first found John. Or maybe a better way to put it would be the day we first found each other. I had just taken another beating. But Dad's attention had turned to Mom, and I ran out the back door before it became my turn again. I climbed up into the tree in our back yard and sat there crying, not taking my eye off of the back door. But it never opened. I guess Dad either wore himself out or exhausted his rage on Mom. Poor Mom.

It was then that I heard what sounded like someone else whimpering. I started looking around but didn't see anything. I climbed down out of the tree to search. I was walking the fence line when I saw him. He was tiny. And scared and shaking. I gently picked him up. "It's okay, boy" I told him as I gently cuddled him and stroked the top of his little head. "It is going to be okay."

From that moment on, we were inseparable. I went to great lengths to hide him from Dad early on because I knew that Dad would haul him off the first chance he got. I decided to name him John, after John Fogerty of Creedence Clearwater Revival. I had heard some of their songs on the radio and liked them. I wanted him to be named after one of the few good things in my life. Mom used to always tell me what a good person I was for saving John, but the truth is, we saved each other. Neither one of us had anyone, and then suddenly, the moment I found him, we both had someone. Those kinds of bonds grow really strong. We have been depending on each other ever since.

But back to the problems I was facing. I was pretty sure that there would be significant medical expenses from the vet, and I was hoping I would have enough cash. We had left Trinidad with a little over $400, and I thought our financial problems were behind us, at least for a while. But money situations and others can change in an instant. This was one lesson life was teaching me fast. I knew I needed to make a plan.

Since we weren't going to be traveling, I felt like we needed some supplies. I couldn't live on crackers and Cokes. I was going to have to buy some kind of pot or pan, and I was going to have to try to figure out how to cook something. For meat, we were going to need some kind of ice chest and matches or a lighter. I could keep hot dogs or bologna in the cooler as long as I had ice. Cheap and simple was going to have to be our motto. And I was going to call Mom and let her know we were okay.

So with some idea of a plan, I headed back into town to the Rainbow Grocery. I bought an ice chest, a small frying pan, some hot dogs and buns, a lighter, and a bag of ice. I also bought a cheap Bible, and on the spur of the moment, an aluminum baseball bat. (The store really did have every-thing.) I had seen firsthand the capabilities of a baseball bat and thought it might come in handy if needed. No more de-pending on John to take care of me. It was time for me to take care of him.

There was a pay phone out front. I picked it up and put in a couple of quarters and dialed home. The operator said I needed to put in two more, and I did. Then the phone rang and Dad answered. I didn't say anything. He said, "Hello" again and then muttered something about damn crank calls and slammed the phone down. Typical of Dad, I thought. Taking money that I don't have and preventing me from connecting with my mom. The fact that I was done with him was just reinforced.

I topped off the tank in the Beetle and debated whether or not to go see John. I was afraid that if I did go, he would be upset because he couldn't leave with me. But I was also afraid that if I didn't go, he would be confused as to where I was. I decided to go back to camp.

CHAPTER 22

BINGO

When I got back to camp, I took stock of what all I had done. I was still very worried about the vet bill, but I knew I was going to have to have even more stuff if John and I were going to survive. If I didn't have enough left to cover the vet bill, I hoped he would just take what I had or let me work it off. There was just nothing else I could do.

I got started trying to build a fire for lunch. I took a bunch of fair-sized rocks and made them into a circle. I found some small twigs and dried leaves and a piece of trash paper by the side of the road. Then I gathered some bigger sticks and logs to throw on the fire once I got it started. I pulled out the lighter, but every time I fired it up the wind blew it right out. I tried to figure out which way the wind was blowing so I could block it with my back. Finally, after blocking the wind and hovering right down over the lighter, I managed to get a small fire burning. I didn't move until it was going pretty well, and then I started adding the smaller sticks. Pretty soon that was going good, too, so I added some bigger ones. I tried to stack them in a way where I could lay the frying pan on top. Once everything was going really well, I tried to make a couple of hot dogs. Best dang hot dogs I had ever tasted.

I let the fire burn down and decided to go for a walk. I found an old bucket I decided might come in handy for putting out fires, and I drew a little water out of the river. Then I went back to camp.

Things were eerily quiet without John there, and I felt terribly alone. I was certain that he felt alone too. I looked over at the Bible. It had blown open, so I picked it up and started reading.

I didn't have much of what the people back home in Center would call 'Bible learnin'. Joel Bookman was not what you would call a Sunday school or church kind of guy. He wasn't the least bit interested in darkening a church door, and most of the people in the town were just fine with that. He didn't want to be around them, and the feeling was pretty much mutual.

The Bible had fallen open to a page called Jeremiah Chapter 29. There were a whole lot of weird names that I could not pronounce, but the best I could figure out was that these people God loved had been captured and hauled off to another place. And they weren't real thrilled about it. But there was one little bit that really caught my attention. God was saying that He knew the thought He had for these people and that He wanted to help them. And if they would just really, really seek Him, they would find Him. That got me to thinking about what had happened yesterday. That Ed guy showed up at the vet's office just in the nick of time. What if, maybe, God had heard my prayers back in Center but was steeling me, building me, and steering me to get me ready for this journey? And what if everything that has happened so far was God trying to prepare me for what's coming next? Maybe He needed me to learn some things before I was ready to handle the next phase. Boy, I thought, some of those lessons don't come all that easy.

I read that Bible for a long while. It was getting on in the day, and I didn't feel like messing with a fire again, so I had a cold hot dog for supper. I figured the bobcat was long gone by then and settled in the sleeping bag ready to call it a night. I heard a noise and a young guy, about my age, came walking up. "Hi," he said in a friendly voice. "Mind if I come in and join you for a bit? Gets pretty lonely out here on the road by yourself. " He had on an old black sweatshirt with a hood, jeans, and a red baseball cap pulled low over his eyes. Everything, including him, was dirty. It had been a few days since he had seen soap and water.

I was wary. I wished John was here. He was always a better judge of people than I was. He would know if this guy was up to no good or not. But the boy smiled again and said, "Looks like you've been travelin' pretty light too. I reckon the vagabonds of this world should try to get acquainted and stick together whenever they get the chance."

That was true enough, I thought to myself.

"Besides," he went on, "I've got a big bag of chocolate chip cookies in my backpack that I would be glad to share."

Cookies. I couldn't remember the last time I had had a cookie. Cookies closed the deal.

"Sure. Come on in. And make yourself at home. I've got some wieners and buns if you would like a cold hot dog."

"That would be freaking awesome!" He almost squealed with delight. "I thought these chocolate chip cookies would take me around the world," he said with a big grin. "Reckon they ain't gonna get me as far as I thought."

We swapped hot dogs for cookies, and when we were through he asked me what I was running from.

"What makes you think I am running?

"Dude! Ray Charles could see you're runnin'."

"You're running, too," I shot back.

He gave me a shrug. "Everybody's runnin'," he said matter-of-factly. "The only thing that's different is how everybody is doing it. Some people got the money to run in style, and the rest of us have to poor-boy it. But everybody's runnin'."

Maybe that was true, I thought to myself. I looked at him again. He seemed very resigned. And very, very cynical.

"So," he said again, "My guess is you are runnin' from hard times and a hard place. Right?"

I nodded.

"Me too. Seems like there's a lot of that goin' around."

We talked for maybe an hour. He was very relaxed and laid back. I began to feel at ease. I think he was grateful for someone to talk to, and I was grateful for someone to keep me from feeling so alone without John. He fell asleep pretty quick and I soon followed.

I woke up early the next morning. The kid was long gone. I was eager to go get John so I packed everything up and left. I was finally on my way to get him. I was headed down the road when suddenly a big deer ran right out in front of me. Instinctively I swerved to miss it and ran off the road. When I did, the VW high-centered. It didn't exactly have a lot of ground clearance and would not budge. I was frantic. *I have to get back to John,* I kept thinking. I had to do something. But try as I might, I could not go anywhere.

Then I remembered what I had read yesterday about really seeking God and being able to find Him. I prayed again and looked around.

Nothing.

My car was probably not visible from the road, so I just stood there by the shoulder for what seemed like an eternity. Actually, it had only been about twenty minutes when a pickup started coming down the road. It had a sign on the door that said, "Colorado Home for Troubled Youth". When it got to me, it stopped and two guys got out. They came over and the driver asked if I needed some help. I nodded up and down.

I led them down to the car, and they sized up the situation and then looked at me. "What the hell were you thinking, kid? You can't go off-roading in no Volkswagen. Are you crazy?"

I didn't say anything. I didn't care what they thought. I was trying to get to John, and they were going to make it happen.

I got in and they pushed and soon I was free. "Can I pay you something?" I asked.

The driver shook his head. "Your money's no good, kid. Just try to use a little common sense next time." They started to walk away, but the driver stopped and turned around. "Hey, you haven't seen another kid around here anywhere, have you? He would be about your age. Wearing a black hoodie and a red cap. He managed to run off from our school, and he's violent and dangerous."

I was immediately torn. The kid I talked to last night was, to me, about as non-violent as they come. I didn't believe these guys for a second. I felt like I was betraying a friend. What should I do? And then I remembered the words of Paul Pearson: "Just try to do the right thing. Try to be a good man. That is the only way each of us can repay the rest of us."

"Yes sir," I said. "He slept right here last night." When I woke up this morning, he was gone. No idea which way he was headed."

Both men looked hard at me. "Then you are damn lucky," the driver said.

I thanked them for their help and then left as fast as I could. I had a rendezvous with a dog!

CHAPTER 23

JOHN

I was worried. Bingo should be here. Today's the day I get out and I expected him as soon as the doors opened, but that was an hour ago. My mind was racing with all sorts of bad thoughts. If I could just get out, I could go look for him. Make sure he's okay. I could—

"He's right back here. Follow me."

Suddenly, there he was. Looking down at me with big ol' tears in his eyes.

"Needless to say, you'll want to keep those wounds clean, best you can. The stitches will dissolve over time. No need to bring him in for that unless they come loose. That's the reason for the cone; so he can't get to them and chew them."

The dreaded plastic cone. I'd had one before when I had gotten neutered. Joel wasn't going to have any dog around humping his or anybody else's leg. *Like I would do such a thing.* Doc opened the door to my kennel, and I slowly limped out. I knew my limitations from being taken outside to potty. No rushed movements. Take it easy. I was extremely sore, and there was terrific pain waiting just beneath the surface. Bingo knelt and looked at me—our eyes just inches apart.

"I love you, John. The past two nights have been the longest of my life. But that's over." Doc attached a short leash (leashes were required inside) and handed it to Bingo.

"So long, son. Holler if there's a problem or if you need anything."

"Thank you, Doc. Again. Thank you so much."

"Glad I could help. His medications are at the front desk."

And with that Bingo turned and headed for the lobby with me close behind. He stopped at the reception desk. A friendly woman smiled and asked, "How's he doing?"

"Doc says he should be fine."

"That's good to hear." She looked down at me. "Isn't it, boy"

Darn sure is.

She smiled at Bingo. "Here're his meds. This one is an antibiotic. He gets it once per day. With a meal. That'll keep his tummy from getting upset. And this one is a painkiller. One tablet as needed and no more than four per day. Any questions?"

Bingo stuffed the bottles in his pocket. "No ma'am."

"And these are your expenses."

Bingo skimmed the paper and landed on the total. $750. Without hesitation he reached into his back pocket and retrieved a wad of bills.

"All I have right now is a little over $400. But I'll pay the rest when I can. I promise."

She smiled. "That will be fine."

He handed her the money. She counted out $400 and handed back the rest.

"You keep this for now. I'm sure you need it."

"Thank you. Thank you very much."

"You're welcome. You two take care now."

"We will."

And with that, Bingo started to remove the leash.

"Oh, that's okay," the nice lady said. "Doc said you can keep it."

"Thank you. He doesn't like them, but it might come in handy."

She smiled, and out the door we went. With my cone bobbing side-to-side. When we got to the car, he opened the passenger door, and I finally managed to climb in once I quit banging the darn thing against the edge. Bingo closed the door, and I settled on the floorboard as he walked around and got in on the driver's side. He started the car and looked down at me.

"Sorry about the cone, boy. But it's for your own good. And mine. We can't afford to have any stitches replaced." He counted the money he had remaining. "We have thirty-two dollars to our name. And a big bill to pay off. I need a job. Let's go look for one. Whatta you say?"

CHAPTER 24

JOHN

The South Fork Visitors Center was situated smack dab in the middle of town at the intersection of Highways 160 and 149. It was a pretty, little building surrounded by small pines and flowers. Bingo thought it would be a good place to ask around about work. He parked the car, opened his door and climbed out.

"You stay here, boy. I won't be long."

I'd never had a panic attack before. Not one. I had heard about them. How terrifying and awful they were. Now I knew. Suddenly, I couldn't breathe. I managed a series of high-shrilled panicked barks.

"Whoa! Whoa, boy! What's the matter? Stop your barking!"

I couldn't.

"It's okay. I'm here. I'm right here! I'm not going anywhere!" He jumped back in and reached over and gently stroked my head inside the cone. "Is it the cone? You've had one before. Or was it my leaving? Are you afraid to be alone again? Afraid I might not come back? You needn't be. I'll always come back to you. I promise."

I was beginning to get my breath back. My sudden

off-the-chart anxiety was slowly fading. I began to relax. I had heard the term "separation anxiety" before but had never really known what it was. Until now. I took a deep breath.

"That's better," he said. "Everything's fine."

And it was.

"Here, let's get this thing off you. But you have to promise to leave those stitches alone. Understand? Of course, you don't. So I'll put this in the back seat for the time being until we need it again."

Oh, I understood all right. And I would *not* be bothering any stitches no matter how bad they itched. I'd had all the vet visits I wanted for a while.

"Come on, you can come with me. Is that what you wanted?"

I barked as he walked around and let me out. It was a darn lot easier without that cone, that's for sure. I gingerly settled on the pavement and followed him in. The sign on the door said, "No Pets Allowed". We kept walking. Inside, a woman behind the counter and another were laughing. They looked over at us. The one behind the counter spoke.

"I'm sorry, you can't bring your—"

She took one look at me and her eyes grew big. So did the other lady's.

"Oh my word. You poor little creature. What happened to *you*?"

"Bobcat got him," Bingo replied.

"Bless his heart. Is he going to be okay?

"Yes ma'am. Doc Worley took good care of him."

"Doc's the best," the other woman said. She was about forty with longish blonde hair and kind eyes. The counter woman was a little older with short brown hair.

Both were now staring at the scrapes and bruises on Bingo's face.

"What about you? Are *you* okay?" the counter woman asked.

"Yes ma'am. It was just a little misunderstanding."

She half-smiled and said, "You new here?"

"We were just passing through when this happened. Looks like we'll be staying a while. And I need a job. I thought maybe you could help me."

"Oh sweetie. I don't know. It's pretty slow around these parts this time of year. Winter is our busy time with people skiing up at Wolf Creek Pass." She looked over at her friend. "You know of anything, Beth?"

The blonde lady shook her head. "No, I sure don't. I'm sorry. Wish we could help you. Where are y'all staying?"

"We're camping just outside of town."

The women looked at each other.

"You're all alone?"

"Yes ma'am. But we're doing fine. Except for the money thing."

The counter lady said, "Well, we'll certainly ask around, and if we come up with *anything,* we know where to find you."

"Thank you. That's very kind."

We turned to go.

"Bye now. Take good care of your friend there."

"I will."

"Oh, I guess we should know your name. Just in case."

Bingo stopped and looked back.

"I'm Bingo and this is John."

We left without waiting on a reply. We'd just about reached the car when we heard, "Hold on! Wait just a minute!" It was the blonde lady. She hurried over.

"How about working for *me*? I own a little souvenir shop just down the road. I can only pay you ten dollars an hour, but after a week you'll have $400. Will that help?"

"I don't know what to say," Bingo answered.

"You say yes. But there is one condition. You go pack up your camping stuff and stay with me. I have an extra room and bath. And I'm a good cook. At least until your dog's better. What do you say?"

I figured Bingo would start crying and was right. "Everything we have is in the car." She threw her arm around him and winked at me.

"Well, then come on, you two. Let's get you settled. And cleaned up and fed."

Music to my ears. And Bingo's too.

"Yes ma'am," he said softly.

"Beth. I'm Beth Gibbons. And it's my honor to meet both of you. I know good folk when I see them."

So do I. And we'd just hit the jackpot with Beth.

"This your car?" she asked.

Bingo nodded.

"Hop in and follow me." We watched her climb into a green Jeep Cherokee and pull out. We got in the Beetle as we were told. Bingo looked over at me.

"What just happened, fella?"

I'd let him work on that. I was concentrating on good food and a soft bed.

We turned up Highway 149, and just up the road we saw Beth motioning to one side. There, to our left sat a small cabin of sorts with a large sign that read, "Beth's Gifts & Souvenirs". She continued past it and a minute later turned off the highway onto a small paved road and another sign that read, "Ponderosa Pines". She drove a ways and turned left onto Fir Street. It was lined with cabins and homes of all shapes and sizes. Hers was one of the smaller cabins but also one of the newest. It was very pretty. We parked beside her in the drive and got out.

"Well, this is it," she said, smiling. "Home sweet home. Come! Have you had breakfast?"

CHAPTER 25

BINGO

The cabin was quaint and charming. It was just what I expected. Sometimes a quick first impression gets reinforced. When we went inside, it was no different. Everything was neat and tidy and elegant. Beth showed me to a bedroom and also to a bathroom. "Now," she said, "let's see about getting you two fed."

We followed her into the kitchen. She opened the fridge and pulled out bacon and eggs and butter and a can of biscuits. A fully stocked fridge, I couldn't help but notice. I looked at John. He noticed it too. Very quickly the aroma of bacon frying filled the kitchen, an aroma that I suddenly realized I missed very much. I went back to the bathroom to wash my face and get cleaned up for the meal. John was already comfortable on the kitchen floor, content to watch Beth cook. It didn't take him long to make himself at home! The fact that John had so quickly settled in and was so relaxed was a good sign. I had been treated with great kindness over the past few weeks, but I had also been burned. I didn't have a lot of confidence in my instincts yet, but I did trust John's.

Very shortly I was treated with bacon and scrambled

eggs and biscuits with butter and red plum jam and a cold glass of milk. A cold glass of milk! Oh my, my. I could really get used to this. I tried not to just scarf everything down, but it had been a long time since I had a home-cooked meal. She tried to make small talk but soon gave up and started cleaning up. I think she was a little surprised by how hungry I was. She cooked another egg for John and sat it and a buttered biscuit on the floor on a small plate for him to eat. A dog's eyes never lie, and the gratitude that John was feeling was easily seen.

Soon we were done. I had eaten almost a whole can of biscuits, and I made sure John got an extra one. I felt stuffed. *This* was eating. What I had been doing mostly on this journey was surviving. All I could do was just keep telling her over and over how good everything was and how grateful we were. She just kept smiling and nodding and telling us not to worry about it.

Shortly thereafter, she left to get back to the store. She told us to make ourselves at home, and if I wanted a sandwich or something to help myself. She said she would be back in a little while to put a roast on so we could have a nice dinner. "You just relax and rest up. Watch TV or something." Then she smiled again. "I think I would also recommend a little soap and hot water."

Point taken.

I looked over at John. He was still lying there on the kitchen floor. I guess he had found his spot. But I also knew that he must still be very tired and very sore. A whole day to just rest there without fear of anything getting him or worrying about the next meal was just exactly what he needed. "Take a nap," I told him. "I am going to go see if I can't rub some of this stink off!"

It is hard to comprehend the medicinal power of soap,

shampoo, and shower until you haven't had those things for several days. It seemed like the fatigue and the anxiety were being washed down the drain with the dirt and the dirty suds. Almost immediately my body began to feel better. It didn't take long for my mind to refresh and my spirit to follow suit. A fresh towel and clean clothes didn't hurt either.

I came back into the living room and saw John was still asleep in the kitchen. There is some rejuvenation going on here for both us, I thought. Rejuvenation that is badly needed. I soon fell asleep sitting up on the couch.

I vaguely heard Beth pop back in at about three to put the roast on and to check on us. She probably looked at us, smiled to herself and said "Perfect!" She was very quiet, and I hardly knew that she had come and gone.

I woke up for good soon after she left and looked around a little bit. There was a nice fenced backyard where John could roam and play and take care of business without worry. One thing I noticed inside the house was that there were very few pictures. There were a couple of pictures each of a young boy and an even younger girl, but that was it. I started wondering what Beth's story might be. How did an attractive 40-something-year-old woman end up all alone in South Fork, Colorado, population less than 400? There was no evidence of any pets, not even a goldfish. It really is none of your business, I told myself.

It wasn't very long until Beth was back home again, this time carrying a couple of bags of groceries. "I figured that since I was no longer just cooking for one, I might better pick up a few things," she explained and went right to work preparing dinner. She seemed genuinely glad to have someone that she could dote over. Or maybe she was just genuinely glad to have some company. Either way, we soon sat down to roast and potatoes and carrots, and I enjoyed my second great home-cooked meal in one day. That was two more than I had had in weeks. And Beth wasn't lying. She was a good cook.

She told me a little bit about the store and what I'd be doing there for the next few days, but naturally the conversation quickly turned to the question of what we were doing in South Fork. I briefly shared our story and filled her in on the highlights of our journey up to now. I left out as many of the lowlights as possible. I was determined not to play the sympathy card.

"Does your mom know that you are okay?" Her tone was rather sharp.

"No. I tried calling once, but my dad answered the phone and I hung up."

"OK," she said. "There is now another condition for you staying here. You must let your mom know that you are all right. Promise me you'll call her."

"Yes ma'am." Then I asked her a question. "I noticed some pictures of a boy and a girl. How did you end up here at South Fork?" John shot me a look. *Don't be any dumber than necessary, Bingo,* was what he seemed to be trying to tell me.

Her bright kind eyes suddenly grew cloudy. Her whole attitude changed. "You don't want to hear my story," she said quietly.

"I didn't mean to pry," I said quickly. "But you are obviously very pretty and very sweet and very kind. I guess I am just a little confused."

She sighed. "I am divorced. The two kids in the pictures are mine. We lived in Orange County, California. My daughter lives in Seattle now and my son in Phoenix. When the kids got old enough to leave, my husband adapted to becoming an empty-nester by spending too much quality time with his much younger secretary. So we divorced and I left. This is where I ended up. The store does pretty well during tourist season and just about breaks even during the off season. My parents have both passed and they left me a little money. And I got a little money when we split everything up after the divorce. So as long as I don't try to live like a Rockefeller, I will be okay. And to tell you the truth, I was tired of trying to live like a Rockefeller. That is a dead end street as far as I'm concerned. And that's the main reason I ended up here. Folks here just don't seem to care about things like that."

"Don't you ever get lonely?" I asked.

She got up and picked up her plate. "I better start getting this cleaned up. We have a big day tomorrow."

CHAPTER 26

BINGO

The store, just like the house, was small, neat, and tasteful. There was clothing and all kinds of little gifts and souvenirs and cards and photos and calendars and things like that. If I am honest I would have to say that none of that stuff had much appeal to me. The morning was rather unexciting. Beth would pop in and out and spent some time visiting with the other store owners there in town. She said it was nice to be able to leave and not have to worry about missing a customer.

She popped back in around lunch time with some sandwiches and chips and soft drinks, and we sat and ate without much conversation. We had barely finished our lunch when a car pulled into the parking lot. "Look alive," Beth laughed. "Your first customer."

An elderly man, probably in his mid-seventies got out of the car. But he just stood there and kinda looked around. I could see a woman in the car. She was about the same age. She looked in the mirror, adjusted her hair and scarf, took a sip from a bottle of water, found her purse, unbuckled her seat belt and then got out too. The man waited for her to come around to the front of the car and then followed her inside.

"Welcome," Beth said brightly. "Thanks for stopping in. Is there something we can help you with?"

The old man shook his head, "We're just gonna browse, if that is okay."

"Sure. Make yourself at home. And please let us know if you need anything."

The woman began to slowly make her way through the store. She took her time, intently studying almost every item on every shelf. The old man just stood off to the side close to me and out of the way. He seemed to have about as much interest in all the things for sale as I did. He looked at me and smiled, "Got a girlfriend?"

I thought about the waitress at the Dairy Queen. "No sir. You don't look like you are having much fun," I said quietly.

"I knew the job was dangerous when I took it," the old man said, smiling. "I'm just doing my job."

"Your job?" I looked at him. "I just assumed you two were married."

"We're married," he said. "Same thing. My job as husband today is to play chauffeur and if, somewhere off in the far distant future, she decides to buy something, it's to be there ready with the credit card. We all have a role to play."

I was grinning a little bit now. I knew he was pulling my leg. His wife was still looking on the same wall. She had maybe moved three feet.

"So you don't mind waiting on her while she shops? I think that's nice."

"Oh, I mind," he said quickly. "But I figure she minded back in the day. Back when I had to work lots of weekends and holidays and crazy hours. I am sure she was never very thrilled about that. So maybe now it's my turn in the barrel. At least that's how I look at it." He paused. "I will tell you this, that is if you are interested in advice from a silly old man," he said as he looked at me. I nodded. "Life is a long and interesting road. It takes you to a million places you never even dreamed about going. The road is hard. Even if you find a good companion. It is a whole lot harder when you find a bad one. A woman you can love will make your life miserable, fascinating, rich, and complete. All at the same time. A woman you can't love will just make your life miserable. You take your time when it comes to picking a woman. This is one decision you have to get right."

He looked over at his wife. She had moved a few more feet. He hung his head. Finally, after an hour or so, she bought eighteen dollars' worth of merchandise. The old man dutifully gave Beth his credit card, took the sack of merchandise and opened the door as his wife went out. He gave us a nod of his head as he left.

"What a sweet couple," Beth said.

CHAPTER 27

JOHN

Following dinner that evening, the three of us took a walk through Ponderosa Pines. There were four main streets in the cozy little neighborhood: Cottonwood, Spruce, Fir and Aspen—along with a few offshoot loops. Several residents were outside enjoying the almost fall-like weather. Beth knew most of them and waved at everybody. They would wave back or shout hellos while eyeing Bingo and me curiously. She did stop to talk to a few, introducing us as her friends from Texas. Interestingly, a great many of the residents were transplanted Texans. With the ever-present aspens, pines, mountains and tranquility coupled with small-town life, it was easy to see why that was. Likely, most had come to visit and either never left or made a hasty return. We even came across a few deer and wild turkeys moseying about on our walk. Normally the race would be on, but I was in no shape to chase anything and was pretty sure Beth preferred I didn't.

That night before bed, as promised, Bingo phoned home. Joel didn't allow Lily a cell phone so Bingo could only try to reach her on their home phone. Just as he feared, Joel answered and he hung up. Maybe next time. It occurred to me we'd been gone from home for about two weeks. July was likely over, and Bingo showed no sign of us turning back. I was fine with that. I didn't miss Joel one iota.

Our second day at the shop was pretty quiet. I think a total of five people came through the door but can't be sure because I spent the day snoozing on a nice comfy bed Beth had made for me from an old rug and blanket.

That night after dinner and another walk, she surprised Bingo with a couple of colorful short-sleeved polo shirts. He tried to pay her for them but she was having none of that. We watched an Adam Sandler movie together on her flat screen TV and ate popcorn. I *love* popcorn. It was great to hear laughs from Bingo again. They had been in short supply for so long, I'd almost forgotten the sound of them. When the movie was over, he and I hit the hay and slept like babies for the second night in a row in the comfort of our bed and the warmth, security and peace of the cabin.

Day three at Beth's Gifts and Souvenirs started slow and never really picked up. Around lunch, Beth returned from running errands and said, "Why don't the two of you take the afternoon off? With pay. It's a beautiful day outside—far too pretty for you to be cooped up in here, that's for sure."

"I couldn't do that," Bingo replied. "Not and be paid for it."

"You can and you will. I'm the boss, remember? Now scoot. And have a good time. Here're the keys."

She handed Bingo the keys to her Jeep and shooed us both outside. After a quick study of the controls, Bingo started it and we pulled away. A couple of minutes later he parked at the cabin.

"I don't feel comfortable driving her vehicle, especially with no license. Let's take the Beetle." And we did. Back at the intersection of 149 and 160 he paused momentarily and then turned right. "How 'bout a drive up Wolf Creek Pass, buddy? Go see what that's all about?"

Sounded good to me. I would have preferred napping on my makeshift bed at the store, but hanging with Bingo will always win out. In no time we were climbing in altitude on the somewhat narrow, winding road. The scenery was beautiful, but I don't think Bingo was noticing. We were already higher than we'd ever been and headed higher. And there was no guardrail. His eyes were glued to the road.

Then it happened. The car began to slow. Much to Bingo's dismay.

"Whoa, what's that all about? What's happening?"

A quick glance told him we had gas. Must be something else. He stomped on the accelerator, and the little car slowed even more. Soon there was a car right behind us. Then another. And behind them, a motorcycle. The one directly behind us, an SUV of some sort, began honking.

"I'm trying! I don't know what's wrong! Dadgumit!!!"

Well, on an anxiety scale of 1-10, the next few miles were off the chart. The cars continued to pile up behind us with no safe place to pass, and now even I was nervous. We passed a short pull-off area. Bingo looked back.

"Dang it! I should have stopped there! What was I thinking?"

Just when I was certain we were headed off the side and straight down to the bottom just so everyone could get by, we reached the Promised Land—the summit. Bingo parked in the first available spot and waited to be jerked from the car by an angry mob. Then we saw. The only one who had stopped was the motorcyclist. Everyone else had continued on past, back down the mountain and on to Pagosa Springs was our guess. Bingo exhaled deeply, got out, let me out, and opened what he thought was the hood, forgetting that on the Beetle, the engine was in the rear. The biker, a big, burly guy dressed in leathers with a full beard walked over and smiled. Bingo closed the trunk, walked around and opened the hood. The tiny engine was a little hot but wasn't smoking or leaking anything.

"Ain't nothin' wrong with your motor," the big guy said.

"'Scuse me?"

"It's fine. It's just that it has an old timey-carburetor that don't like this thin mountain air, that's all. I'm not a fan of technology for the most part, but electronic fuel injection is one of the greatest inventions of our lifetime. I even have it on my hog."

His "hog" was a gorgeous midnight blue Harley Davidson with chrome you could wash your face and brush your hair in. Bingo looked at him and smiled.

"Thank you. I was certain we were on our last leg."

"Well, you're not. And even if you were, I wouldn't leave you here till the problem was fixed and two of you were back on the road. Can't say the same for those other folks though. The name's Cy."

"Very nice to meet you, Cy. I'm Bingo and that's John."

Cy smiled and said, "Well, hello, John. Hope you got the best end of that deal, whatever it was. But I'm not sure you did."

"Bobcat," Bingo said. "And no he didn't. But he tried."

"Well, give me one of those any day of the week. Win or lose. That's somethin' not near enough folks do these days. *Try.*" He looked around. "Want me to take a pic of you both there by the sign?"

"I don't have a camera," Bingo said. "Or a phone."

"Well, I do. Y'all get over there."

We did as we were told, and Cy took our picture on his smartphone.

"Judgin' from the plates on your Bug there, I'm guessin' you don't have a permanent address in these parts either. Would that be accurate?"

Bingo thought for a moment, recalling Beth's home address. He hesitated and then answered, "No sir, we don't."

"Then I'll keep the photo to remember you by. Anything else I can do for you?"

"No sir. We're just gonna walk around a little and head on back down."

"Don't get in a hurry goin' down. Your car's gonna be sluggish again at the start, but it'll get better as you go. And speakin' of go, I'm gone. Goodbye, gentlemen."

"So long, Cy. Thank you for stopping and helping us."

The big man waved over his shoulder, climbed on his bike, pushed the start button and pulled away. We watched him go. Bingo looked at me.

"I don't know about you, boy, but I've got to pee."

He wasn't alone. With no one around, we exited the parking area and hid behind some pines while a car passed by headed back the direction we'd come. When we were done, we explored a few minutes; I decided I needed to poop; and then we headed back to the car. With the ski lodge closed, there wasn't much to see or do. So we drove back to South Fork.

CHAPTER 28

JOHN

We got back to the cabin in time to switch vehicles and pick Beth up at closing time. Bingo shared the details of our adventure over supper. After another neighborhood walk and movie, we all called it a day. Staying there felt strange. We were made to feel so welcome by this woman we hardly knew, it seemed we'd been there for weeks rather than days. To say it felt like what I imagined home life should feel like is the best I can come up with. I know Bingo must have been experiencing the same feeling. I wondered how long it would last.

Because we canines have that famous sixth sense about people, I knew Bingo was gold the first time I laid my puppy eyes on him. He had no sooner discovered me when I felt the love already oozing out of him. And he had so much to give. So much pent-up inside. I thank my lucky stars for allowing the two of us to cross paths. I might have been okay on my own, and maybe even with someone else, but I don't think I'd ever have been treated with such care and devotion. And if that wasn't enough, Bingo gives fantastic tummy rubs. And always takes the time to wipe the sleep out of my eyes and keep my toenails clipped (although I'm not crazy about the latter.) And when I was sick with something called Vestibular Syndrome, he never left my side. He even slept outside nestled close to me. Vestibular Syndrome, if you don't know, is where a dog's eyes move back and forth, side-to-side really fast. And they don't stop. As you can imagine, this wreaks havoc with trying to see and stand, much less walk. And can last for days. Mine lasted two weeks. And the worst of it was the constant nausea. I remember just lying still with my eyes closed hoping it would stop. At Bingo's urging, I managed an occasional sip of water and a small nibble or two of food, but that's it. When the symptoms finally did ease, I walked with my head tilted at a forty-five degree angle for another week. I'm told I looked like the RCA dog but don't know who he is. It was another month before I could walk in a straight line and felt completely normal. I can't imagine going through that without Bingo there with me. And of course, he's always there to console me at the presence of thunder, sirens and fireworks or such. I remember hearing him and Lily discussing it one day, and she said she read somewhere that he shouldn't do that because consoling a dog at a time like that only reinforces the dog's perception that there *is* a problem or something terribly wrong. Thankfully, he didn't buy that. And I'm glad. I need that reassurance.

And one of my favorite things is this (don't laugh): Like all dogs, I like to roll over on my back and stretch out. And whenever I do that, he says, "You're not big, but you know what? You sure are long. You are a long dog." I just love that.

What I don't like is him tickling me, which he loves to do. My whiskers, the inside of my ears and worst of all, the little tufts of hair between my toes. That drives me crazy. And he just laughs. Oh well, a small price to pay for winning the lottery. So to speak.

The next morning he and I were enjoying pop tarts for breakfast just before heading to work when Beth asked, "Do you fish, Bingo?"

"Just once for catfish with my dad," he said softly. "It didn't end well. And we never went again."

Didn't end well was an understatement of grand proportions. Upon returning home that day, Bingo couldn't bring himself to clean the fish, and as expected, Joel became furious. He beat Bingo and then stood over him and made him behead, skin and gut every single one—Bingo crying the whole time. But it was Joel's words that hurt Bingo the worst. A boy can only hear he's pathetic and worthless and that no father on the planet would want him just so many times before he begins to believe it.

"Well, if you'd like, I can arrange for the two of you to go fly fishing this afternoon with a good friend of mine. Randy Sales owns Hidden Lake Outfitters just east of town. You might have seen it on your way in the other day. His is one of the best fly fishing shops in this part of the state, and Randy is one of the most knowledgeable and sought-after teachers and guides in all of Colorado. Not only that, but he and his wife Sharon are two of the nicest people you will ever meet, trust me. Whatta you say?"

"I think I'd like that a lot. But I don't want you paying me when I'm not working, like you did yesterday."

"You let me worry about that, you hear? You two just have fun."

CHAPTER 29

BINGO

I must admit I was very nervous. I knew nothing about fishing, much less fly fishing and this guy who was taking me fished for a living. I was sure he had taken movies stars, politicians, and all kinds of fancy people fishing. And now he was taking me. I felt completely out of place. I had visions of trying to cast and the fly catching me in the butt. Or, worse yet, ripping my ear off. I was doing a great job of talking myself out of going when Randy pulled up in front of the shop. Like everyone else around here, his F250 was four-wheel drive. John and I went outside, he stuck out his hand and we all did the introduction thing. Then he told us to get in and that we were going to have great fun today. John hopped right in. He was getting better and spryer by the day. He was starting to be his old self again and I was glad for that.

We made small talk on the way. Randy was about forty, clean-shaven and dressed in very nice jeans and a shirt with the name of his shop on it. He asked about my fishing experience and knowledge, and I guessed he was trying to figure out what lay in store for him and whether or not he had a long day ahead. I watched him pretty intently, and not once did I ever see him roll his eyes. We pulled up by the river just outside of town, and he started unloading all the gear. The first thing he had me do was slip on some waders. Then we carried everything down to the bank. He looked at John. "I know you want to jump in the river and splash around, but you'll just scare the fish off. We're gonna need you to hang out on the bank."

I looked at John and laughed. The wagging tail suddenly dropped. He deflated like his balloon had just burst. "Come on now," I said. "The stitches are almost gone and you are almost healed up. Let's don't be any dumber than necessary. No stupid chances, okay?"

Once we got everything situated, Randy presented me with a fly rod and reel. "This is an Orvis Clearwater 9 ft rod and an Orvis Clearwater IV reel with 8W line, very good equipment. If we are going to do good work, we need to have good tools." He showed me how to hold it with my thumb on top of the shaft and the reel just behind my wrist. He said the rod needed to be an extension of my forearm. He explained that he wanted me to load the rod twice, once going backward and once going forward. I gave him an obviously confused look because he stopped and laughed. "What I mean by loaded is that the rod bends. When it bends, it stores energy. When we bend the rod, we load it with stored energy. Understand?"

I nodded affirmatively. *If you say so*, was my unspoken thought.

He said the tip of the rod needed to travel in a straight line back and through and not to turn my body. "Just use your forearm and wrist. Smooth motions, a nice easy rhythm. Bring it back and pause. You pause to let the line start to catch up. Just before the lure gets all the way back bring the rod forward. The line will fly out ahead of you.

Think railroad tracks he told me. Parallel lines. The tip of the rod will follow the inside track, and the lure will follow the outside track. Remember," he emphasized again, "load the rod on the way back, pause, and load the rod on the way through. Now here. You try it."

I actually did not do too bad. I didn't snag any part of my body with the lure.

"See," he said enthusiastically, "piece of cake. Just practice a little."

We waded a little farther out into the river. There was a big boulder sitting in the water near the south bank. The boulder deflected the current, and the water moved slower behind it. Randy pointed it out and said that would be a good place to try to cast. That lots of times fish will sit there and rest and feed. "Go ahead," he said, "give it a shot."

I tried to remember everything he said. I was concentrating with all my might. I got nervous and stiff and gave what I thought was a mighty cast. The lure landed about four feet up on the river bank.

Randy cackled. "Congratulations," said with a very good nature. "You just missed the river!"

I smiled bleakly. John, who had laid down in the sandy gravel just off the water's edge, was giving me that confused head twist thing that only dogs can do. But Randy was quick with the encouragement. "Don't worry about it," he said. "No problem. Nobody is born knowing how to do this. Everybody has to learn. Give it another shot."

I at least hit the river with my next cast. It wasn't exactly where I wanted it, but it was in the water. I let out a big breath of relief. He then told me to slowly pull the line back in, keeping the tip low to the water. He watched me maybe a half dozen more times. I managed to get the lure a little farther and a little closer to my target each time.

"I think you're getting there," he told me. "Just relax and have fun. I am going to move a little farther up the river. You're doing great."

Pretty soon he had caught a couple of fish. I had not even gotten a nibble. I suck at this, I thought to myself. But just then I felt a good tug. I jerked the rod back. I had about ten feet of slack line like Randy had taught me, and I started to reel it in. The fish pulled against me as hard as he could. Randy, who had now come back over, said to let him run a little bit but not to let him have slack. "Use your trigger finger." he said." "Use that to keep slack out of the line!"

Finally, I began to bring the fish in. He started to tire, but not before he had resisted with all his strength. What a proud, magnificent struggle, I thought. Finally, I had him close enough, and Randy was there with the net. With a quick swoop, a fourteen inch rainbow trout was my first catch of the day.

Randy was ecstatic. John was barking on the river bank. To tell the truth, I was more relieved than excited. "The first one is the hardest," Randy told me. "You're on your way now." He seemed genuinely excited for me.

But I was really too intense to be excited. I was too focused on trying to do everything right to unwind enough to enjoy the moment. I stayed that way for the next hour or so. I even caught a couple of more fish, but I was still so focused on what I was doing, I couldn't ever relax.

Then, just as I was getting ready to make another cast, it all changed. I raised my rod to start back and suddenly caught a glimpse of the sunlight dancing on the ripples. It was like the water was shimmering. It almost took my breath. I looked around. The water was pure and clean and clear and cool. It was just starting its long journey to the Gulf of Mexico. I wondered what adventures lay ahead for it as it marched toward the sea. Would they be anything like what John and I experienced?

For the first time, I stopped and looked around. There was a stand of aspens just behind us, with their leaves rustling gently and their white bark shining in the bright day. The hills around us wrapped us in our little cocoon and made us feel secluded and far away from anything or anyone. A hawk soared high overhead. Downstream a mama antelope and two little ones cautiously got a noon-time drink. It was so peaceful and so beautiful. What am I doing? I have been so nervous and so uptight that I haven't even been able to enjoy what should be a wonderful day.

Right then and there I quit worrying about technique and whether I was doing something wrong. I quit worrying about what Randy thought. I spent the rest of the afternoon just being. I just wanted to be alive, to breathe free clean air and to soak in as much of the beauty of my surroundings as I possibly could. I stopped even caring if I caught another fish or not. Being here, being alive, being part of this—that was enough for me. I was going to enjoy it.

The rest of the day flew by. I probably caught eight fish. No telling how many Randy caught. I stopped keeping track. He released all of them except for a couple which he said would be plenty for dinner that night. Soon the sun began to dip behind the surrounding hills. Darkness comes early in a small sheltered valley. We loaded everything up and headed to Randy's house.

CHAPTER 30

BINGO

Randy and his wife Sharon had a beautiful rustic cabin a little north of South Fork cut way back into the mountain with a stand of pines on one side and aspens on the other. A small stream ran right by the back porch. It was a log cabin, but it was tight and warm and secure with lots of pretty paneling and wood on the inside too.

Sharon greeted us at the door. She was gorgeous with long auburn hair and green eyes. She reached down and gave John a good scratching behind the ears. Instant buddies. She told us to make ourselves at home, so I plopped down on a huge leather couch that almost swallowed me. John settled at my feet. "I am going to drop back into the kitchen," Sharon said. "It will only take Randy a second or two to clean the fish, and then I'll fry them up. Everything else is just about ready."

Sure enough, we soon sat down to a fabulous meal of pan-seared trout, covered in butter and lemon sauce, roasted potatoes, fresh green beans and homemade biscuits. It was fabulous. John got a small piece of fish and a biscuit. He was starting to really like biscuits. It was plainly evident by how he perked up anytime he heard the word.

Sharon wanted to know all about our day. I told her about completely missing the river on my first try, and she laughed. But, she quickly pointed out that we had caught enough fish for a good dinner, and that was what mattered. And it probably wasn't too bad being outside all day.

After we had eaten and talked the day to death, Randy got up and excused himself. Soon he was back with the fly rod and reel I had been using. He laid it gently on the floor beside the table.

"I do this for a living," he began. "And I have done this a long time. I've had the privilege of going fishing with movie stars, rock stars, athletes, senators, and lots of powerful people. And we have shared a lot of laughs. But almost all of them have just been on a trip to feed their egos. They are trying to catch more fish or catch bigger fish. It is all about status. And I suspect it's that way with just about everything in their lives. The competition and the power and whatever is necessary to make them look and seem bigger is all they seem to care about."

He paused and looked straight at me. "I watched you all afternoon. You wasted half of it trying too hard to do everything right. You were so worried that you might mess up and so concerned about what I might be thinking, that you couldn't enjoy yourself at all. It might have been for a different reason, but it was the same result as with all the rich guys. But something changed with you, and I saw it instantly. You finally connected to everything that was going on around you. When you stopped making everything be about you and your insecurity, that's when you got it. That's when you figured it out. My job is not to help people pull fish out of a river. That is not why I do what I do. My job is to help them live, to notice that life is going on all around them and realize they are not the center of the universe.

None of us are. Any time I can make that happen, is a very good day for me."

He stopped and picked up the fly gear. "And that happened with you today. And when it did, you became a fly fisherman. That's why I want you to have this rod and reel. It served you well today, and I trust it will continue to do so for many, many years."

Sharon smiled proudly. I didn't know what to say. I had no idea how much that stuff cost, but I knew it wasn't cheap. Even I knew this wasn't a twenty dollar Zebco you bought at Walmart. All I could do was mumble a very sincere *thank you* for the gear. And for the day. And try not to cry.

Randy then took us back to Beth's house. I almost said took us home. When we got there, Beth wanted to know everything, but we were both very tired, and she let us go with a promise from us that we would not leave anything out tomorrow morning over breakfast.

We went to our room and quickly got ready for bed. I turned out the lights and stared at the ceiling or a minute or two. "Dang, John," I said out loud, "I am beginning to think we could get used to this."

CHAPTER 31

JOHN

Beth got the complete lowdown on our fishing trip from Bingo over their breakfast of cereal and toast the next morning. Sadly, I was back on dog food. "I knew you'd like Randy and Sharon," she said. "I'm really glad you went."

So were we.

When we got to the store, I took my usual place on my bed near the cash register. It was Saturday, and business was pretty good. The big sellers were caps and T-shirts. Mostly the plain, colored shirts with just South Fork, Colorado, printed on the front and nothing on the back. Beth had some pretty elaborate ones, but they weren't selling today. Same way with the caps. The basic, no-frills ball caps were a hot item. Especially brown and blue. Before we knew it, Beth was calling it a day. She opened the register, removed some bills and handed them to Bingo.

"Here you go—$400 for a forty-hour week. Just as I promised."

"No, I—"

"Not up for discussion. Take it."

Bingo slowly reached out and took the money. "Thank

you, Beth. So much."

"You're welcome. Let's lock up and go home. I don't know about you two, but I'm hungry."

I barked.

She laughed and said, "And there's someone else who is."

"He's always hungry," Bingo smiled.

I won't argue that.

As soon as we got back to the cabin, Bingo headed for the car.

"There's some place I have to go. We won't be long."

"OK," Beth smiled. "Dinner won't be ready for a while."

And with that, we climbed in the trusty Beetle. A few minutes later we pulled up at the veterinary clinic.

"Come on, boy. We've got business to take care of." And in we went.

The only customer was an elderly woman with a cat in a small kennel. I, of course, knew better than to investigate closer. I followed Bingo to the counter. The woman seated behind it smiled at us.

"Can I help you?"

"Yes ma'am. I'm here to pay the rest of my bill. My name is Bingo."

"Oh yes, I remember you." She looked down at me. "How's John doing?"

"Great. Thanks to Doc."

"That's good to hear. Let's see. . . ." She looked at her computer screen and smiled. "Looks like your bill has been settled."

"Settled?"

"Paid in full. You don't owe anything."

"What? Who paid it?"

"Doctor Worley. His initials are by the balance. Which

clearly reads zero."

Bingo's eyes had begun to fill. "Can I see him?"

"I'm sorry. He's in surgery at the moment. Will be for a while, I'm afraid. Would you like me to leave him a message?"

"No ma'am. I have to tell him in person."

"I understand. I'll tell him you dropped by."

"Thank you." Bingo turned, walked a few steps and stopped. "Ma'am?"

She looked up. "The fella who called Doc the night I brought John in. Do you know who it was? I think his first name was Ed."

"Sure do. That was Ed Brannigan. We all love Ed. He's such a sweetheart."

"Can you tell me where can I find him?

"I sure can. Just follow 160 for a mile or so east and then just past the Mountain Aire RV Park you'll see a dirt road going north. No sign. Follow it about a mile and you'll come to Ed's cabin. It's the only one there. Can't miss it."

"Thank you."

I followed Bingo back out to the car. We found the RV park, dirt road and Ed's cabin in short order. His red pickup was parked out front. We parked beside it and got out. We heard a noise coming from a nearby barn and walked over to it. The inside looked more like a workshop than a barn. Ed looked up and saw us. He was wearing an old pair of old coveralls and boots.

"Well now, if it's not the modern day *Travels with Charley.*"

"'Scuse me?"

"*Travels with Charley.* By John Steinbeck. The book he wrote about him and his dog travelin' across the country together. You two remind me of them." He wiped his hands on a rag from his back pocket and shook hands with Bingo.

"I don't know that book," Bingo said.

"It's a good one. Give it a try sometime." He looked at me. "Appears your buddy is healin' up nicely. That's good. What can I do for you fellas?"

"Yes he is. And I—we—came to say thank you. For stopping to help us that night. I couldn't remember if I ever really thanked you. That night is still pretty much a blur."

"Well, that's awful nice of you. And you're welcome. The both of you. Come, sit down." He led us to an old picnic table near the cabin. The wood was in pretty poor shape. "Can I get you fellas somethin' to drink? Some water or tea?"

"No thanks. We've got to head back for supper pretty soon."

"That's right. Y'all are stayin' with Beth Gibbons, aren't you?'

"Yes sir."

"Couldn't have picked a finer woman."

"Actually, she picked us. Took us in and gave me a job at her souvenir shop."

"Course she would. That's Beth. Won't find a purer heart in the county. Wait here just a minute, I have somethin' for her." We watched him head back inside the barn. He soon returned with a large, odd-looking item made of iron and colored glass in the shape of flowers and butterflies. "She's already got a couple from me, but one can never have too many suncatchers."

"It's beautiful," Bingo said. "Did you make it?"

"I did. That's pretty much all I do these days."

"So you're retired?"

"Yes sir. Forty-five years with the county public works department, installin' and repairin' people's water wells. These days I drink a lot of coffee, make these things and look out for the good folks of South Fork. I'm also on the city council."

"Have you lived here all your life?"

"I have. Born and raised. And you? What's y'all's story? If you care to share."

"I don't like to talk about it much. The short version is we ran away from home."

Ed looked at the plates on the Beetle.

"Texas is a far piece."

"Sure is." Bingo was growing sad. Ed noticed.

"I have a younger brother who left home when he was about your age. I'd rather not say why other than he was just young and stupid. Today he's a successful businessman in Denver. If he can make it on his own out in this world of ours at that young age, you can. And he did it on half a brain and didn't have anyone backing him up. You, on the other hand, appear to have all your good sense, *and* you have John there. You're gonna be just fine, son. I just know it. Might be here. Might be someplace else a long ways from here. But you're gonna light in the right place one day and know it when you do. Trust me on that."

Bingo's tears had returned. Poor kid. His heart just wasn't big enough for all the feelings he had pent-up inside him. Something had to give. More often than not, it was tears. Ed stood, touched him on the shoulder and walked to the barn. He returned with another suncatcher. This one, pocketsize. He handed it to Bingo. It was in the shape of a small moon and stars above a tiny cabin.

"Sometimes we don't choose our home, son. Sometimes, home chooses us."

Bingo stared at the ornament, thinking. He then stood, nodded, picked up Beth's suncatcher and walked to the car, sobbing. I followed along, sneaking a quick glance back at

Ed. He was smiling. And inside, so was I. Bingo slowly turned the car around and pulled away. After we'd gone a short ways he stopped.

"What did I do to deserve this, John? What did I ever do to earn all these people's kindness? I wish I knew."

He sat for a moment, then reached up and hung his little cabin suncatcher from the Beetle's rear view mirror.

CHAPTER 32

JOHN

We got home just as Beth was setting the table. Bingo had regained some semblance of normalcy and after washing up, we were greeted with a supper of spaghetti and garlic toast for them and dog food for me. Afterwards, Beth passed on our evening walk, and he and I headed out the door. Bingo didn't say much as we walked that day, but that was okay. We were just headed back toward Beth's cabin when we heard it. A dog. Howling in pain.

We both looked down the road before us and saw a man yelling at and beating a dog with a tree limb. The poor thing was chained and couldn't get away. Bingo took off in their direction, but I quickly passed him. My attempt to knock the man down failed (I wish I were bigger), so I tore into the first thing I could latch onto. His leg. I managed several good bites before Bingo pulled me off.

"That's enough, John. *Leave it! LEAVE IT!*" he yelled.

I did as I was told. Bingo freed the dog, a young black lab, from the chain and it scampered away, whimpering, its tail between its legs. The man climbed to his feet, took one look at us and limped toward his pickup. We watched him open the driver's door and then saw it—a rifle hanging on a rack in the window. Bingo turned and ran as the man reached for it.

"Run, John! RUN!"

And we did. As fast as we could. Not pausing to look back but instead, nervously listening for the shot. None came. We were both exhausted when we reached Beth's cabin and burst inside. Beth was seated on the couch, working on her cross-stitch. She looked up, eyes big.

"What is going on?"

Bingo told her.

"Are you two okay?"

"Yes. We're fine."

"Tell me again which cabin it was."

Bingo described it and the location.

"Ollie Stevens. Doesn't surprise me one iota. He's about as worthless as they come. Been wishing he'd move for years. And I'm not alone."

"What're we gonna do?"

"Nothing right now. We'll just see what happens."

It didn't take long. Twenty minutes later we heard the sound of a vehicle in the driveway. Bingo peered through the blinds.

"Who is it, Bingo?"

"The sheriff."

"That so? Well, you go on out there, and I'll be along in a minute."

I followed Bingo outside. A man climbed out of a large black pickup with *Rio Grande County Sheriff* printed on the sides. He was about sixty and dressed in khaki trousers and matching shirt. He walked over and looked at us.

"What's your name, son?"

"Bingo, sir."

"And the dog's?"

"John."

The sheriff suppressed a smile and said, "I guess you know why I'm here."

"He was hurting that dog!" Bingo cried. "*Bad*. We had to do s*omething!*"

"I understand. But attacking a man on his own property is another matter. I'm afraid I'm going to have to take the dog until I can get this all sorted out."

"Please, mister. Don't do that. We've been through a lot. And we need each other. Please don't take him."

"I'm sorry, son. But ol' Ollie is plenty upset. And has a right to be. Your dog got him pretty good."

Wish I'd gotten him better.

"Can I come? And stay with John?"

"No, son. Not right now."

"Hello, Sheriff. What brings you to these parts?"

He smiled and said, "Hello, Beth. I'm guessing you have an idea."

"Sounds to me like Ollie got what he deserved. He's been mistreating those animals of his for years."

"Beth, please."

"How's Margaret? She still painting?"

"She's fine. And yes, she is. She's moved on from landscapes to portraits. Said she'd love to do one of you."

"And I'd love that. I'll give her a call."

"She'll be tickled. Now, can we just—"

A white Honda Pilot pulled into the drive. We all watched the driver climb out.

"Why, hello, Sheriff. Haven't seen you in a while."

"Hello, Doc. What brings you here?" The sheriff turned and looked at Beth and smiled. "Wait, let me guess."

"Just heard a friend of mine was in some sort of

misunderstanding and thought I would come and see if I could help."

Before the sheriff could answer, a Cadillac Escalade pulled in. A couple got out.

"Dadgum, Beth, did you phone the whole town?"

"No. I didn't have time, Sheriff. But if you don't mind waiting. . . ."

"That won't be necessary." He turned. "Hello Randy. Sharon."

"Howdy, Sheriff. How goes it? Caught any keepers lately? I hear they're really moving over by Lookout Point."

A familiar bright red pickup pulled in. Beth smiled, hurried over and opened the driver's door.

"Hello, Ed. What a wonderful surprise. Haven't seen you in a while."

Ed Brannigan smiled and climbed out. "Hello, Beth. Just in the neighborhood and saw all the vehicles. What's goin' on here?"

The sheriff threw up his hands. "Okay, I give up. I know when to surrender. I consider you people the finest South Fork has to offer, if you don't know that already. And friends of mine as well. The dog can stay. But this isn't over. I can probably persuade Ollie not to press any formal charges, but he's going to want someone to pay for any medical expenses and property damage, you can count on that."

"Forget the medical expenses," Beth said. "Ollie isn't about to go see a doctor. He doesn't trust them. And how bad can the bites be anyway? Heck, we've all probably been bitten at one time or another. Especially Doc."

"Yes I have. More times than I can recall. And I'm still standing."

"Exactly what property damage are you referring to, Sheriff?" Randy asked.

"His torn jeans."

Randy smiled. "We'll buy him a new pair. Several. He needs some, that's for sure."

The sheriff looked at Bingo and smiled. "Son, best thing a fella can have in this world is a good friend. Looks like you've got yourself a handful."

Bingo nodded but didn't speak.

"I gotta get going."

"To talk to Ollie again?"

"No, that can wait. Margaret was just setting the table when he phoned. Tonight's chicken and dumplings and I'm starving."

"Sheriff?"

"Yes, son?"

"What about him hurting that dog? Can't you do something about that?"

"That's tricky, son. Unless he's caught in the act."

"*We* saw him."

"I know. And I'm going to caution him about it. Strongly. In the meantime, do you have a leash?"

"Yes sir, Doc gave me one when John was hurt."

"Well, we don't have any law around here saying you have to use one, but you might think about it. We can't have this happening again."

"Yes sir."

"Remember, the man *was* hurt. That can't feel good to you."

"Truth is, Sheriff, I'd rather see people hurt than see an animal of any kind harmed," Bingo said softly.

"Yeah, I guess I feel that way myself sometimes. I gotta go. So long, everybody."

Everyone said goodbye and watched him leave. Doc Worley walked over and knelt beside me.

"His wounds are healing up nicely. Looks like you're going to be just fine, John. Just don't make a habit of biting people. Even if they do deserve it."

I barked and everyone laughed.

"When's the last time he had a rabies vaccination, Bingo?"

"Six months ago. He hates collars, so I keep the tag in my stuff."

"That'll work. He's good to go for another eighteen months. I've yet to see the disease in a bobcat, but raccoons and skunks are another matter. Watch out for those."

Bingo stepped forward. "Doc, I haven't had a chance to thank you in person about my bill. I don't really know what to say. You're so kind. Everybody's so nice."

"You're welcome, Bingo. My pleasure. Now, don't any of the rest of you go getting any ideas that I'm running a charity clinic, I'm not. I just recognize a good cause when I see one."

Everyone laughed. Beth looked over at Ed.

"Ed, bless your heart, what *are* you doing here? I didn't call you."

"I did," Randy said. "Right after you phoned me. I remembered he and the sheriff go way back."

"Yes we do. I've known Joe since first grade."

"And, the way I heard it, if it weren't for you, we might not even all be here right now."

"You heard right," Doc replied.

"I'm thinkin' someone else had a hand on my wheel that night," Ed offered.

Beth smiled. "Of course He did. That's a given. Now, who wants pie with ice cream? I just took one out of the oven—apple."

Sharon walked over. "Bingo, honey, if you know what's

good for you and John, y'all best move over here out of the way or risk being trampled. The lady does know how to bake a pie."

Everyone laughed, and we moved aside with Sharon, then joined everyone inside. She was right. Beth can flat out bake a pie.

CHAPTER 33

BINGO

As I lay in bed that night, I tried to process a few things. My mind was pretty much racing from everything that had happened that day and over the past two weeks. A lot had happened to us since we hit South Fork and so there was a lot to try to wrap my head around.

First, there were some changes going on with me. Regular balanced meals, a soft warm bed and regular hygiene were starting to take effect. I felt healthier. I looked healthier. I was no longer just skin and bones. I was beginning to fill out and put on a few pounds. And that did not even begin to take into account the effect of not having all the stress and fear of worrying about tomorrow or being afraid of the next beating was having on my emotional welfare. I had never really even known what it was like to live stress free, even for just a few days. My attitude, my outlook, and my mood were improving daily.

John, too, was benefitting from a regular diet and stable home life. He had just about completely healed from his round with the bobcat. I could see that we were going to be just fine. And from the way he went after Ollie, his mental health and sense of right and wrong were as strong as ever.

We had it good. No question about that. The people of this town were amazing. They had gone out of their way to help us and to make us feel welcome. But that was making me a little uneasy—no, maybe unsettled was a better word. There was something going on here, something that I wasn't seeing or at least understanding. I finally drifted off to sleep, but it was a restless night. Since I had never had it good, maybe I was having a hard time dealing with good.

Monday at the store was slow. Maybe ten people walked through the door with the largest sale of the day being $37. There was no way that the revenue being produced and the workload required would justify paying me for eight hours. That only added to my general concern. Beth, of course, was cheerful and unconcerned, so I did not press it. After work came another good meal and another walk with John, thankfully peaceful this time. While brushing my teeth, I did notice that I was looking rather shaggy. I hadn't had a haircut in a couple of months. Mom had always cut my hair before. She had an old pair of shears, and the only haircut I had ever had was a short burr. I kinda liked having a little hair, although it needed a little TLC for sure. I also was beginning to have a good start on a beard, just one more indication that changes were going on with and all around me.

On Tuesday morning, Beth asked me to stay home and not go to the store. She said she was having firewood for the winter delivered, and it would really help her if someone was here when they brought it. I told her that was no problem at all and was actually quite glad to be doing something useful. Soon after she left, a truck and trailer showed up with a full load. That's a lot of wood, I thought to myself, but I guess it gets pretty cold here in the winter. The driver came over and asked if I wanted it stacked. He said it was an extra $75 for him to stack it. I told him no, I would do it. At last I could actually earn some of the money I was getting paid. He said that was great with him and that he was just going to drop the trailer because he had a bunch of errands to run. "Take your time, kid," he told me. "No hurry at all."

After he unhooked the trailer he said, "Oh, by the way, we didn't get all of this split like we wanted to. She may have to get someone to split some of it for her."

I can split firewood, I thought to myself as he drove away. I had seen where Beth kept her axe and thought I could be really be useful to her, so I went to work.

I would have to say that splitting and stacking firewood would not be my dream job, but I was determined to give back to Beth because all she had done was give to *me*. After just two minutes of swinging that axe I was completely out of breath. I had to stop and put my hands on my knees and allow my lungs to catch up a little. I am not fighting a fire, I reminded myself. Strong and steady. It is going to be a long day.

John, on the other hand, seemed to be enjoying this, although he did get up and move a little farther away after he had watched me swing the axe a time or two. He seemed to have a rather bemused look on his face the whole day.

I worked all day, and I was just finishing stacking the last of the wood when Beth pulled up. "Awesome," she beamed proudly. You get inside and get cleaned up. This deserves a big dinner."

"Actually, maybe just a sandwich," I suggested. "I am just too tired to be hungry."

She laughed and those bright eyes twinkled. "Go on inside, you two, I've got this. I'll put the tools away."

A hot shower helped a lot, but it did not wash off all the tiredness. When I walked into the living room Beth had a big fire going even though it was not cold outside at all. "A man should enjoy the fruits of his labor," she told me as she brought me a BLT. "Just sit back and enjoy." She also handed me a couple of Tylenol. "Take these. They will

help you feel better in the morning." Then she disappeared into the kitchen again and returned with a big mug of hot chocolate. Once again, she had the solution. "This always helps me to relax," she said, sounding just like a mom.

After the hot chocolate, she said she wanted to catch up on some reading and told me to just lie down on the couch. The Tylenol was starting to help a little bit but I was still very tired and starting to get stiff and sore. I watched the fire for a while, and the last thing I remember thinking was that I probably needed to get back to school whenever I got the chance. I was sure I did not want to do what I did today for the rest of my life.

CHAPTER 34

BINGO

When I woke up the next morning, the sun was fully up and Beth had already gone to work. I tried to sit up. Every movement produced a new ache. I sure was glad I took those Tylenol. I wouldn't want to try to move without them. There was a note on the table along with two more. "Take these," the note said. "And I made you an appointment with Diana this morning at 11:00. She's our local hairdresser. She's really good and you need some shearing. Then take the afternoon off and rest those muscles! Her shop is just south of the Visitors Center. Can't miss it. No dogs allowed."

Once I could get up and start moving, around some of the stiffness and soreness began to ease a little bit. And the Tylenol started kicking in too. I put John in the back yard and headed to the hair salon a little early.

This, too, was a new experience for me. Diana seemed really nice and motioned me to a chair. I sat down and she turned me around and slid the chair back to where the back of my neck was resting against the edge of a sink. She then lathered my hair with some really great smelling shampoo and gently massaged my scalp with her fingernails. It felt amazingly relaxing. I tried to resist the urge to fall asleep. But soon she had me rinsed off and transferred to another chair. "So what are we going to do today?" she asked hopefully.

I had no idea what to tell her, so I just said, "Can you make something out of nothing?"

She laughed and said, "Let me ask you a question. Do you think there are some pretty attractive people around here?"

"Now that you mention it, I guess there are."

"You're welcome. Making something out of nothing is what I do for a living."

I laughed and we made small talk while she snipped away, and then I tried to get to what had been bothering me for the last couple of days.

"Could I ask you a serious question? Ever since I have been here," I went on not waiting for a reply, "people have been so nice to me. Too nice. Beth took me into her home and gave me a job when she had known me all of two minutes. Who does that? Randy spent a day fishing with me and then gave me what I am sure is a pretty expensive fly fishing outfit. The vet forgave me a $350 bill that I owed him. Normally people are suspicious of strangers. These people treat me like I am some kind of prince."

The snipping stopped and she spun me around to where I was looking right at her. She had a deadly serious look on her face. "First of all, these are really good people. Really great people. But there *is* more to it than that. A couple of years ago we lost a kid here."

"Oh, no," I said softly. "Cancer? Car wreck?"

"No, not lost like that. There was a young boy who came from a bad home. No mom, and his dad was just mean and ornery. He beat that boy and we all knew it. But nobody said anything and nobody did anything. And the boy turned mean and started doing all kinds of bad things. The state finally had to take him away and put him in a home for bad kids. Every one of us felt just terrible. We felt like we let that boy down, that we had the opportunity to help him, but we didn't. When you came along, I guess everybody just saw you as a second chance."

That explained a lot. I felt a little better. She finished up and gave me a mirror. I did look quite a bit better. "Now go to the store and buy yourself a razor and some shaving cream."

"Yes ma'am. How much do I owe you?"

"On the house," she said. "I reckon I need some atonement too."

I left and headed to the store. I was trying to decide on which razor and shaving cream to buy when Ed walked in. He saw me and walked over. Just as I was picking out my stuff, he placed a tube of after shave cream in my hand. "Trust me. You're gonna want this," he smiled. I thanked him and headed to the register.

I paid, told Ed goodbye and started to leave when Ollie came barreling through the door. He saw me and snarled. Ed quickly stepped between us. "Lucky you can hide behind an old man," Ollie growled at me.

Ed got right in his face. "You can blame everybody else for your problems all you want, Ollie. But the fact is you were beatin' them dogs. And you shouldn't be doin' it."

Ollie just pushed on by. "I got rid of them dogs," he said. "Just a bunch of damn useless, worthless mouths to feed."

The hair on the back of my neck stood up. I had heard those exact words before from Dad and I knew. I mean I just knew. *The father of the boy that they lost was Ollie.* And the boy that had spent the night at my camp was Ollie's son. I wondered why he had come back. Was it to try to reconcile with his dad? Or seek revenge? Either way was a dead end street. I hoped he had decided to put it all behind him and was moving on.

I was pretty quiet at dinner that night although Beth just kept going on and on about how much better I looked. I didn't say anything about the other boy. I figured if she wanted to talk about things she would. And I was still tired and sore. But that night as I lay in bed, I wondered what would become of him. And I thought how lucky I was that I had gotten the benefit of a town's guilt over something that had happened before. I wonder if that is how this works, I thought to myself. I wonder if God can take all of these bad things and somehow work it all for good to benefit not just me but lots of other people as well. I thought about the Bible I had bought. Maybe I should start reading that thing more. Maybe it would help explain some of this stuff.

CHAPTER 35

JOHN

The next day, Randy stopped by the shop shortly after lunch.

"Boss Lady, I was thinking I'd borrow your workers this afternoon if that's okay. I've been told the fish are practically jumping in the boat up at Pool Table Lake. Whatta you say?"

"OK with me." She looked at Bingo. "Whatta you think?" she smiled.

Bingo smiled big and said, "Come on, boy. We've never been in a boat before!" And we headed for the door. Outside sat Randy's pickup with a small aluminum boat trailered behind it."

"I thought you'd have a big, fancy boat," Bingo said, as we climbed in.

"Don't need one for the kind of fishing we're going to do. Pool Table's not very big. Plus the road's not too wide."

We made a quick stop by the cabin so Bingo could get his fishing gear and then headed west out of town toward Creede. After a handful of miles, Randy pulled off the highway at a small green sign that read, "Pool Table Lake", with an arrow pointing the way. The road quickly changed from

---

paved to dirt and abruptly narrowed. We started up a severe incline, and Randy gave it the gas, the tires searching for traction on the washboard-like dirt and rocks. Then the road got seriously narrow and steep. Like me, Bingo was watching with attention. Or, I should say, tension.

"Uh, have you been here before?" he asked nervously.

"Oh, yeah. Many times."

"What happens if we meet someone coming the other way?"

He smiled. "One of us backs up."

That didn't sound good to either of us.

"How far to the top?"

"Not too far. Don't worry. I haven't gone over the edge yet." Another smile.

An eternal few minutes later, we rounded a final sharp curve and were greeted with a big, beautiful, open, flat area. In it, a few trucks and trailers looking out over a small, pristine blue lake. After that drive, it looked like Heaven on Earth. In no time, we were on the water with Randy at the oars. He turned them over to Bingo and pointed. "That's where we want. Right over there."

I must admit to being rather uncomfortable. The gentle rocking motion of the boat beneath my feet was not one I had experienced before, nor was thrilled with. Eventually, I reached a happy medium of security. Of sorts.

The days had certainly begun to cool some, and it was very pleasant. There wasn't a single breeze, and after my fascination with my reflection in the water began to fade and I was confident we were not going to capsize, I curled up in the middle of the boat out of each's way. There, I lay listening to their soft voices and feeling the rhythmic motions of their casts. It wasn't long before I was on the cusp of sleep.

"You can try any of those flies you want," Randy was saying "But I'd stick to the ones in that first little tray there. Those will work best here."

"How come?" Bingo asked.

I don't recall Randy's exact reply. I think it had something to do with native bugs or something. I then thought I heard talk of baseball and girls but am not certain. My mind was elsewhere. In my dream, Bingo and I were back on the road in the VW at night slowly chugging along in a terrible snowstorm. The only lights on the landscape were from the Beetle's barely sufficient headlights. Finally, in the distance we spotted the dim light of a gas station. A few minutes later we pulled in. *Open*. Thank goodness. We climbed out and went inside. A kind, older gentleman smiled at us from behind the counter. It's crazy to say, but he looked a little like Ed. And Randy. And Doc Worley. Bingo smiled back and was about to ask his name when we heard the jingle of the bell above the door. We both turned and looked straight into the eyes of Joel Bookman. He was holding a blue aluminum baseball bat raised high above his head. He smiled and swung it. An electric shock went through me.

"Whoa, boy! Settle down! *You'll turn the boat over!*"

I suddenly felt familiar hands on me. Trusted hands. I awoke.

"Dadgum, buddy. You scared the crap outta me."

"And me," Randy smiled.

"What'd you do, have a bad dream?"

I darn sure did. I'd had some before. Sometimes Bingo would wake me and say I was running in my sleep, my legs going lickety-split. But none as bad as this one. I sat up, looked around and realized all was right with the world.

The fishing went on for another hour or so. Plenty were caught by both. All were released. Finally, we headed back to shore. Once everything was in place, we started back down the mountain. Thankfully, we met no one and despite several feelings that we were sliding off into oblivion, we didn't. When we were safely back to the highway, Bingo turned and said, "Thank you, Randy. I had a great time."

"So did I. Thanks for coming."

Bingo looked over at me. "That was different, wasn't it, buddy? What'd you think of the whole boat thing?"

I hadn't fully decided. It was definitely different. I kept quiet.

"Bingo, what would you think about working afternoons for me in my shop? Cleaning, stocking, whatever I need. Beth and I have discussed it, and she's okay with it."

Bingo smiled and nodded. "I'd like that. Very much."

"Cool. We'll start tomorrow."

Bingo stared straight ahead, trying hard to control his emotions. He actually did a good job of it. Like his, my heart was soaring. A lot was being piled on Bingo's platter these days, and it was all good. And long overdue.

CHAPTER 36

JOHN

The next day, Bingo quickly settled into his new work routine. Talk about a kid in a candy store, Randy's shop had everything a fly fisherman, novice or expert, could ever need or want. Rows and rows of reels costing hundreds of dollars and rods of all kinds—fiberglass, graphite, carbon fiber and bamboo—ranging into the thousands. There was a whole separate room housing hundreds of lures and flies and the equipment and supplies for making one's own. And another for clothing and accessories. As Bingo learned the ropes, I spent the afternoon on the front porch, greeting customers and enjoying the weather.

Randy gave Bingo Saturday afternoon off because Beth had planned a trip to Creede for the three of us. On the way, Bingo pointed out the road to Pool Table Lake and asked Beth if she'd ever been there.

"No sir. Sandy, my friend from the Visitors Center, and I started up it one day to see the lake, and halfway up met a big truck and trailer. He wasn't about to back his trailer up the mountain, so you-know-who had to back down. He wasn't happy because it took me nearly an hour. Sandy was white as a ghost and never said a word the whole time.

Once we were safely down, you couldn't pry my hands off the wheel. I wasn't able to use my fingers for a week."

Bingo was dying laughing. "I'm sorry," he said. "But I know what you're talking about. It scared the daylights out of me too. And John."

Yes it did.

Beth smiled. "I never even look at that sign. If I never hear those three words again, it'll be too soon."

Same here.

Creede was only twenty-five miles from South Fork and as she drove, Beth told us a little of its history. It seems it was one of the last boomtowns during the Silver Rush in the late 1800s. Then, it had a population of 10,000. Today, a little less than 300. These days it's home to the nationally famous Creede Repertory Theatre and has been for over fifty years. Beth said she and Sandy regularly attend their wonderful plays there and looked forward to taking Bingo when the new season opened.

"Sorry, John, no dogs," she smiled.

No problem.

It wasn't long before we pulled into town. Our first stop was an outdoor eatery called "Bob's Dogs".

"Hungry? These are the best hot dogs around. And Bob is a sweetie pie. Come on!"

She led us to a small, and I mean *small*, bright red building resembling a roadside fireworks stand. A heavyset, balding gentleman turned from the grill and smiled.

"I thought I heard your familiar, sweet voice. Hello, Beth."

"Hello, Bob. I've been telling my friends here you're the mountaintop when it comes to hot dogs, so make me look good now, you hear?"

He smiled big. Bob had one of those smiles that just

warmed you all over. It did me, anyway. "Two combo specials?"

"Three," she answered, winking at me. Did I mention I had fallen in love with this woman?

"Yes ma'am. Three comin' up. What to drink?"

"Two Cokes," she said, looking at Bingo, He nodded and she added, "and one bottled water."

"Be just a minute."

She paid and led us to one of the small, round picnic tables with chairs. All appeared to have been repainted recently. Ours was bright blue. I moseyed off to pee and had no sooner returned when Bob arrived with our food. Bingo makes a really good hot dog, but I have to say Beth knew what she was talking about. Judging from the mustard on Bingo's face, it was clear he agreed. Discussion had ceased and didn't pick back up until the last of our dogs (wonder where they got that name, anyway?), fries and drinks were gone. Leaving the car parked there, we walked downtown.

And what a pleasant walk it was. Plenty of new smells, friendly people, and even another dog or two along the way—also friendly. She paused in front of a small shop called "Lost in Time Crafts and Antiques".

"I love this place," she said. "Jennifer always finds the neatest stuff. Come on, dogs allowed."

We followed her in, and after introductions I followed Bingo straight back to the rear where something had caught his attention. We arrived to find a brightly lit nook of used books.

"I miss reading, John," Bingo said. "I want to see if I can find a good book or two to read at night. He had no sooner said that when he turned and smiled at me. He pulled a small orange and white paperback from the top shelf and held it up. "What are the chances? *Travels with Charley* by

John Steinbeck. This is the book Ed was telling me about! And look—just three bucks!"

Did I ever mention that my absolute favorite feeling in the whole, entire world is seeing Bingo happy? Even if it's just for the briefest of moments. The sight of pure joy on his face sends something coursing through me I simply can't describe.

He hurried over and excitedly showed the book to Beth, then paid for it. She purchased some earrings made by a local artist, and we went our merry way. I didn't know if someone was smiling down on us at that very moment or not. I just knew our good days had seriously begun to out-number our bad.

That night in bed, we hit the road with Mr. Steinbeck and Charley.

CHAPTER 37

BINGO

Sunday was to be a big day. Ed was picking me up at 8:00 a.m., and we were headed to Denver to catch a Rockies afternoon game. Ed had cleared it with Beth, and he was right on time. John was going to hang out with Beth all day. I didn't think he would mind too much, and Ed and I were going to make a full day of it.

"Thanks for taking me to the game," I said as soon we took off.

"No," Ed replied. "You are doing me the favor. I love goin' to ballgames, but it's four and a half hours to Denver, one way. I don't really like makin' such a long trip all by my lonesome."

"I've never been to a sporting event."

Ed grinned that big grin of his. "Then you are in for a treat. You're gonna love it. Know much about baseball?"

I nodded affirmatively. "I watch sports on TV quite a bit. Just never got a chance to go." Sports was a very good escape for a young boy who desperately needed a place to hide. I left that part unsaid.

Ed wasn't kidding about the drive. It was every bit of four and a half hours. We stopped once to get gas and

---

stretch our legs. A quick trip to the restroom, a Coke and candy bar and we were on our way again. Ed said we would eat a lot at the game.

The drive was pretty uneventful except for the scenery. I had set out to see a mountain. I saw a bunch that morning. Beautiful soaring peaks so white they looked like clouds. Thick forests that I knew had to be teeming with wild life. Beautiful clear streams that ran right beside the roadside. It was almost too much to take in and certainly too beautiful to describe.

We parked and bought our tickets. By then it was 1:15 and we had forty-five minutes before the game started. That was fine with me. Ed got us some peanuts and another Coke. Coors Field was huge—the biggest building I had ever been in. We had good seats along the first base line. I hoped I might get a foul ball. I watched the players warm up, but mostly I watched all the people as the stands began to fill. I wondered about their stories. I wondered how many of them were wondering about mine.

After a few innings, Ed got up and motioned for me to come with him. We walked over to the bleachers high above left field. There was a restaurant there he said had great burgers. As always, Ed was true to his word. We dined on big cheeseburgers with bacon, gigantic onion rings and milkshakes so thick that we had to use a spoon. Then we headed back to our seats.

The Rockies were playing the first-place Dodgers. The visitors turned a couple of Rockies errors and a couple of home runs into a 5-1 lead going into the bottom of the ninth. The Dodgers came out with their outfielders deep, determined to keep everything in front of them. The first and third basemen hugged the lines. The first Rockies batter hit the ball sharply, a towering fly to center field, the deepest part of the ballpark. But the centerfielder, already playing deep, had no trouble settling under it at the warning track. Out number one. The next batter took the first pitch. The pitcher was trying to nibble at the corners and missed. Ball one. The next pitch was high and tight. Right under the chin. Universal pitcher language that said, "Don't get too comfortable up there." The batter backed out and shot the pitcher a look. But now the count was 2-0 and the pitcher did not want to walk this guy. He had to make a good pitch. The batter laid down a perfect bunt, a slow roller down the third base line. With the infield back, the third baseman had no chance. The batter was safe without even drawing a throw. Now things were starting to get interesting. The runner at first drew a big lead, drawing a throw. He took an even bigger lead, and the pitcher gave him a long look before coming home. The runner took off and the batter hit a screaming line drive right over the shortstop's head. It was right between the center and left fielders who sprinted to run it down. The runner never slowed down and scored all the way from first with the batter safe at second. Now it was 5-2 with a runner in scoring position and one out. The next batter came through and lined a single into right. The runner on second scored standing up as the throw came into second to hold the hitter at first base. It was 5-3 now, with one out and the tying run at the plate. The crowd was really into it now. The pitcher went into his stretch, checked the runner and came home. The batter took a mighty swing, but got on top of it and meekly grounded the ball to the shortstop who turned it into a double play. Ballgame. We headed for the exits.

CHAPTER 38

BINGO

When thirty-five thousand people exit a ball park at rush hour in a major city, things are going to get snarly in a hurry. We inched along as traffic crawled.

"This is almost as bad as Dallas at rush hour."

"Ed's eyebrows shot up. "Almost? If there is somethin' worse than this, I don't want no part of it." But eventually things thinned out, and we began to move. It was getting dark, and the conversation began to lag. I wanted to ask Ed about Ollie and his son but decided against it. Evidently Ed had something on his mind, too, because he was the one who broke the silence.

"You never did tell me why you left home. Obviously things weren't great or you wouldn't be here. What is your story, Bingo?"

I shrugged. "Just didn't get along with my dad, I guess."

"I kinda figured that," Ed said nodding. "But you don't seem bitter or angry. Meanness can lead to lots more meanness. I've seen it first-hand. How come it didn't happen to you?"

"I never knew my grandpa, but my mom said he was real

mean to my dad. And my dad was real mean to me. I did not want to just carry that along. Like you said, meanness can lead to more meanness. I wanted that to stop. Plus I had my mom. She loved me. She didn't do much to help me, but I could always tell that she wanted me to escape from all of that. And I had John. Never underestimate that. He was always there and always making me laugh and keeping me sane. I don't know where I would have ended up without him."

"Well," Ed said gently, "I ain't tryin' to pry. But if you ever want to talk about it, I got big ears."

"I don't much like to talk about it. I can't talk about it without it sounding like I am feeling sorry for myself, and this world does not need any more pity parties. I just try to do the best I can. I figure there are lots of people who have it worse off than me."

"True enough," Ed said. And then we drifted back into silence.

Just as we got home Ed said, "Remember this. That last batter, he swung at the first pitch. All the smart guys who write for the papers are gonna say tomorrow that he was dumb for swinging at it. If he had hit a home run, those same smart guys would be talking about how gutsy and courageous he was. That's what we love about sports. Every result is quickly apparent. It ain't that way in life. Sometimes the results of our decisions don't show up for weeks or even years. Life is gonna throw you some wicked curve balls, and you're gonna look pretty foolish at the plate sometimes. But you're gonna get some pitches to hit. The trick is to keep swinging. The worst thing you can do is to walk back to the dugout without ever takin' the bat off your shoulder. You remember that."

"I will." I shook his hand and thanked him again for a

great day. Then I ran inside to play with John. He seemed very glad to see me, although I suspected that he had a pretty good day too. Very quickly I settled into a deep and peaceful sleep, the crack of the bat and the roar of the crowd echoing through my dreams.

CHAPTER 39

JOHN

Monday was another slow day at Beth's shop but not at Randy's. He explained that his business boomed throughout the warm months, slowing only during winter and ski season when Beth and most businesses in town were at their busiest. That was good because Bingo preferred to stay busy. That night in bed, he continued *Travels with Charley*, something I'd been looking forward to.

"You know," he said, "Steinbeck was a real famous writer. I might've named you after him if I'd read this book back then. Don't worry; your name would still be John. Anyway, the book is also called *In Search of America*, and for *their* trip, he outfitted his truck with a big camper shell. And listen to this—on the inside he had a double bed, stove, heater, refrigerator, lights, a chemical toilet, food, water, dishes and pencils, paper, notebooks, a typewriter and some of his favorite books. Holy cow. That puts our little VW Beetle to shame. Oh, and he gave his truck a name—painted right on the side: Rocinante—the name of Don Quixote's horse. I'm not exactly sure who Don Quixote is, but I'm sure he was someone famous." *I didn't have a clue either.* "You know what? I think we should name the Beetle. I don't want to paint it on the side or anything, but it should be called something." After thinking about it briefly, he smiled and said, "How about *Olivia?* It's only fitting, don't you think? I know Al would be proud."

The following evening after supper, Bingo and I took a walk around Ponderosa Pines while Beth went down to the Rainbow Grocery in search of some new winter boots. (I'm telling you, that store has everything.) Summer wasn't officially drawing to a close, but it was already starting to feel like it. The evenings were cool and the deer and wild turkeys were growing more abundant on their visits to the neighborhood. We passed several of each as they wandered about. Some still eyed me cautiously, but most paid us no mind. We rounded a corner with Bingo going one way and me the other. He stopped and looked back.

"What're you doing? Come on, let's go this way."

I held my ground.

"We don't want to go that direction, remember? You-know-who lives down that road."

I didn't move.

"Seriously?"

I sat down.

"OK, but let's keep moving and not dilly-dally around. You hear?"

I waited for him, and just as we were passing Ollie's cabin he looked up and saw what I'd seen. *FOR SALE.*

We stopped. It appeared Ollie was long gone. His tiny cabin was dark and quiet. I looked up at Bingo. He was lost in thought, his mind racing. Then he began to talk, never taking his eyes off the cabin.

"Holy cow, buddy. It's small and in need of repair, but we don't need anything big and fancy. And I can hammer and paint. Maybe we live here. We can't stay at Beth's forever. I could get a better job—a full-time one that pays more. Maybe I can rent it until I can afford to buy it. It's beautiful here. And peaceful. And we have friends here. Maybe. . . ."

His voice softened and then changed.

"Who am I kidding? What about school? I have to finish high school first. I can't work full-time anywhere until I do. And we'll need money for other things—food, clothes, utilities, firewood, everything. What was I thinking?" He paused, staring at the cabin, then turned and looked at me. "Let's go, buddy." Then he walked away. I followed him back to Beth's. She greeted us at the door.

"Have a good walk? Look what I found! Not very swanky but they're functional. And that's all I care about—keeping my feet warm." She held up her new winter boots. "We'll need to get you some, but we still have plenty of time. They have a good assortment in your size. Now, who wants desert? I stopped off at the Mountaintop Bakery on my way home and got six of their famous apple fritters baked fresh this morning. Just need to warm 'em up a little."

We all ate fritters (I was given the smallest one), watched a little TV and Bingo excused himself and called it a day. I could tell his mind was elsewhere. He passed on reading and went straight to bed. An hour or so later, I dozed off. Then, around midnight, I was awakened by the worst sound in the whole world. Bingo crying.

He sat up, sobbing. "I'm scared, John. What am I doing? What am I *looking* for? Al told me not to stop until I found it. And I don't even know what that is anymore. It's like the world is turning around and around, and I'm on the outside looking in. Where do I fit? I don't know. But one thing I do know—as much as I like it here, this isn't where I belong. This is not where we're meant to be, you and me. I don't know how to explain that to you. I just have this feeling something is tugging at me. Pulling me hard—away from here. It has been for a while now."

Suddenly Beth was at the door. "Bingo? Everything all right? Are you two okay?"

He swallowed hard. "Yes ma'am. We're fine. Really."

"Are you sure?"

"Yes ma'am. I'm sure."

"OK. You let me know if you need anything, you hear?"

"Thank you. We will."

Once she was gone, he buried his face in his pillow and cried even harder. I was sick. I crowded up against him as close as I could. To say it was a long night wouldn't do it justice.

The next morning, Bingo showered and dressed in silence. I followed him downstairs. Beth was at the coffee maker, pouring herself a cup. She looked over and saw the backpack in Bingo's hand. Her eyes filled.

"Please tell me you two are just going hiking or something."

Bingo dropped the satchel and walked over, crying. She took him in her arms.

"I'm sorry," he said, his face buried in her shoulder. "I owe you so much."

"You don't owe me a single thing. Not even an explanation. You'll never know the joy the two of you have brought me."

Both were bawling now. And they did for a while. Finally, she let go and stepped back. "I love you, Bingo. You two will *always* have a home here. You know that, right?"

He looked at her and nodded.

"Do you know where you'll go?"

He shook his head, still unable to speak.

"OK. The thought of the two of you just wandering aimlessly is more than I can bear. You need a destination. Everyone needs a destination. I want you to go to Kalispell. It's in Montana. My sister lives there. Her name is Kate. I've told her all about you both and she would like very much to meet you. *And* she has something to show you. Something you need to see. I'm going to write down her address, and I want you to promise me you'll go see her. Will you do that for me?"

"Yes ma'am. We will. I promise."

Beth scribbled the address on a yellow Post-it note and folded Bingo's fingers around it. "Don't you lose that," she said.

"I won't." He tucked the note into his jeans pocket, hugged her again and walked to the door. "Will you do something for *me*?" he asked softly.

"Anything."

"Please tell Doc and Ed goodbye for us."

"I will. What about Randy?"

"I'm going to tell him myself."

She smiled and nodded. "Goodbye, love."

"Goodbye, Beth."

And we left.

CHAPTER 40

JOHN

As we drove away, I sat, thinking. Even though I comprehend what goes on, I don't always understand it. I guess it's that way with people too. I loved Beth. And that place. And I would have loved to stay. But I love Bingo more. And want what's best for him. And if meant leaving, so be it.

A few minutes later, we pulled up at Randy's shop. A couple of SUV's were parked out front. We peered through the door and spotted Randy with a customer. He saw us, excused himself and came out to the porch.

"What's up, guys?" He noticed the red in Bingo's eyes. "Something wrong?"

Bingo summoned all his strength and said, "We've come to say goodbye."

"That so?"

"Please don't ask why. I'm not sure I can tell you."

Randy nodded. "Beth know?"

"Yes sir."

The two hugged.

"Thank you for everything you've done for us."

"You're welcome, Bingo. And I'm not going to try and

change your mind. I can see it's made up. I guess I can even understand it a little. Least I think I do. I was your age once. But that doesn't make it any easier. I am damn sure going to miss the two of you." He looked down at me. "Well, John, it certainly was a pleasure meeting you. Bingo's lucky to have you."

"Randy?" Bingo said softly.

"Yes sir?"

"I wish you were my dad."

Randy's eyes glistened. He swallowed hard and said, "Oh, buddy. I—"

"No, I didn't mean *that*. I know that's not possible. What I was trying to say was, I wish my dad could've been more like you."

Who was it that sang that song about grown men crying? Tim McGraw? Well, he was right. They do. And goodbyes are hard. They wear on you. Even if you are a dog. I thought I was tougher than a keg of six-penny nails, but I was quickly reminded I'm not. I squeezed past Bingo and made my way to the car. Bingo and Randy hugged one last time, and Bingo walked over and we climbed in. I'm certain Randy was waving goodbye from the porch, but neither of us looked back. A few miles down the road, Bingo had recovered somewhat and pulled over. He reached over, opened the glove box, pulled out his trusty map and sat studying it.

"Kinda what I thought," he said. "Kalispell is a *long* way from here. All the way up by Glacier National Park and the Canadian border. It's still August so we should be okay with the weather. And I have nearly $800 saved up, so we're not hurting for money. We better get going, buddy. We've got a promise to keep."

CHAPTER 41

BINGO

And so, just like that, we were on the road again. I was kicking myself for getting so emotional. What a sap, I told myself. While I was growing and filling out physically, I realized that emotionally, in too many ways I was still a young boy, timid and unsure. And I was unsure right now. I had just left the best thing that had ever happened to me. Kind people who genuinely cared about me and wanted to help support me and nurture me were now in my rear view mirror. And in the windshield was more uncertainty, more challenges, and many more unknowns. I had no high school diploma, no driver's license, and no last name. What a sap, I told myself again. And what an idiot.

I beat myself up for a good hour. When you are being abused from the outside it is very easy to abuse yourself from the inside. There is always that nagging feeling that somehow this was all my fault. The insecurity and despair and doubt had always been with me, and it flared to the surface like hot lava in unsettled moments. I was in a fierce battle with my demons, and at the moment, they were on the verge of overwhelming me.

I looked at John. He was lying comfortably in the

passenger seat—his eyes on me. He could see the tempest raging inside me. Sometimes I thought he knew me better than I did. How could I do this to him? Not only was I throwing myself into the unknown, but I was taking John along with me. What right did I have to unseat John from the best situation that he had ever had too? *Maybe I should have left him with Beth,* I thought for just a second, but dismissed that idea immediately. We were inseparable. We would be miserable without each other. Wherever we were headed, whatever we were racing into, we would face it together. Just like we had faced everything else before. The simple truth was I didn't think either of us could make it on our own. I knew I couldn't.

Slowly, I began to regain some control. My fears and doubts did not disappear but they did become smaller. I knew I had to go. I had no idea why, but I knew it was time to move on. I knew there was more waiting for me. I kept thinking about what Ed had said on the ride home from the Rockies game. Every hero can become a bum, and every bum gets a chance to be the hero. I knew I couldn't just stay safe, wrapped in the cocoon of the kindness of South Fork. It was time for me to get the bat off my shoulder and start taking a few cuts.

The day was bright and warm, but not hot. We had the windows down and the wind flowed through the car making the ride quite pleasant. This was Colorado and the scenery was terrific. I relaxed even more. We had made it this far. We could keep going.

Up ahead I saw what looked like someone sitting on the side of the road with their face buried in their hands. Instinctively, I felt that someone was in trouble. I began to slow down and pulled over. The person looked up. It was a girl just about my age. My experience with girls my age had been fifty-fifty on this trip, so I became very cautious. I had already been suckered once. Keep your guard up, I reminded myself.

"Are you okay?" I asked.

"Yeah. I'm okay," she said softly.

I could see how pretty she was.

"I've been walking all morning and needed to rest for a minute."

"Why are you walking?"

"I'm going to Grand Junction."

"But why walk? Why not take the bus or something?"

Her bright eyes grew cloudy. "I guess I had to leave in a hurry."

"We're going to Grand Junction," I blurted out. "Want a ride?" Idiot, I thought to myself. You have walked right into it again.

She got up and warily approached the VW. She seemed afraid of us. Then she saw John, and the light returned to her eyes. John's presence seemed to reassure her.

"What a pretty boy," she said gently as she stroked John's back.

I looked at John. He had been a good barometer this whole trip, and I decided to check the weather. He was up and his tail was wagging enthusiastically. That was good enough for me. "Get in." I said. "I bet John won't mind hopping into the back seat."

"No, no, no," she laughed. "I'm not going to make *him* move. I'd rather ride in the back anyway!"

John seemed more than okay with that arrangement. As soon as we got her boarded, we took off. Everybody's mood picked up.

"What's in Grand Junction?" I asked. I had a hard time seeing her, but I could see that she was very pretty. She had on hiking boots and shorts and a T-shirt under an unbuttoned flannel shirt. I was struck by how wholesome she looked.

"I was about to ask you the same thing," she said, laughing easily.

"You first."

She sighed. "My Memaw lives there. I'm going to see her."

But why the hurry to leave? I wondered. Why not just call her grandmother to come get her? I thought of the words the kid (Ollie's kid, I was sure) had said that night at the campsite: "Everybody's runnin' from somethin'."

"OK. You've told me where you are going. But what are you getting away from?" I could see her studying my face. "It's okay," I assured her. "We are getting away from something too."

She decided to open up. "I guess you're okay. I guess I can tell you about this. I sure need to tell someone."

I cut her off. "Who am I going to tell? I don't know anybody you know. Your secret is safe with us."

"My mom has a new boyfriend. He's rich. He bought her a new Range Rover. He's taken her to Europe. And he wants us to come live with him in Denver. He has a big house there with an indoor swimming pool. And a cabin near Creede. That's where we were when I left. After my mom and dad got divorced, my mom struggled. We went through some hard times. This guy is instant security."

"Maybe I'm stupid," I smiled, "but I am not seeing the problem."

"When Mom's not around, he wants to like me the same way that he likes Mom."

"Ohhh." The light was beginning to come on. "Have you talked to her about it?"

"I tried, but she doesn't want to hear it. She said it was either my imagination or my fault. I think she's afraid of losing him."

"Suddenly she ducked down in the back seat as a Lexus SUV came up behind and took off around us. "That's him! He's looking for me." He sped on up ahead.

"Man that is wrong. I am so sorry. What about your dad?"

"He has a new wife. She's only a few years older that I am. She's why my parents got divorced in the first place. They don't seem to want me around much."

Then she turned things around to me. "So what's *your* story?"

CHAPTER 42

BINGO

I filled her in, but just the highlights mostly. She seemed incredulous that we would leave South Fork. "But," she said smiling, "I am sure glad you did."

I felt a hunger pain. I looked at John. He was always feeling hunger pains. So I turned back to her. "Are you hungry?"

"Umm, I don't have any money."

"I do. And my name is Bingo. And this is John." I finally remembered not to make the same mistake I made at the Dairy Queen.

"I'm Alicia. And I don't have any money for gas."

"That sure is a long last name," I teased. "I think we'll be okay. On both gas and food. My treat. We are grateful for the company." It was then that I realized that I had completely forgotten about feeling so low.

"In that case, there's a place in Montrose called the The Cabin or The Log Cabin or something like that. Memaw always stops there. They have the best chicken tenders."

"OK. Chicken tenders it is. Montrose, here we come." It seems we made it in no time.

The Cabin was good. I could see why her Memaw always stopped there. She got the chicken fingers, and I got a big cheeseburger and fries. Did I mention that I like cheeseburgers? John got a giant corn dog which he woofed down in a few bites. "Maybe try chewing next time, John." Alicia laughed. I liked it when she laughed.

While we were eating, she looked at her phone. She said it was a good thing she had put it on silent because it had been going off like crazy. Then her bright eyes began to tear up.

"What's wrong?" It was obvious that something was.

"There's this girl at school. She saw me talking to her boyfriend right before the end of the school year. She got all mad, and she's been posting videos calling me a skank and a slut all summer. She just posted another one. We were just talking about math homework, I swear we were. I don't want her stupid ol' boyfriend!"

She looked down again and started to cry. "I just want things to go back to normal," she said, sobbing softly. "Is normal too much to ask?"

I didn't say it, but returning back to what had always been my normal was the last thing I wanted.

We piled back in Olivia and headed toward Grand Junction. Pretty soon the darkness had all passed, and she talked and chatted and sang and kept us entertained the whole way. We hit Grand Junction about 3:00 p.m., and she knew the exact way to Memaw's. She begged us to come in because she knew that her Memaw would want to meet us and thank us, but I said no. I felt like we would just be in the way. So she gave me a big hug and started for the door. Then I heard her say, "Oh, what the heck." And she turned around, ran back to me and gave me a big kiss. Then she headed back toward the door. I sat there hoping, but this time she didn't turn around.

I looked over at John. He had an unmistakable *Oh, no,*

here we go again look on his face. If it was possible for dogs to roll their eyes, I am pretty sure John just did it. I looked in the back seat. There was a note that had her name and phone number and message that said please call me. As I drove away, I saw her waving from the window.

Down the road a ways, we spotted a Walmart. I asked John if he was ready to ride in the buggy again. I felt like we needed a few things, and I wanted to pick up stuff to make sandwiches and a bag of ice. And on the spur of the moment, I got a small tent just big enough for the two of us. Once back in the car, we headed north. My plan was to go west on I-70, but that fizzled. All westbound traffic on the interstate was closed due to a jackknifed eighteen-wheeler, we were told. So I fell in with the rest of the traffic going east, figuring I'd turn back north first chance I got.

I reflected on the day as I drove. Why I felt so driven to leave that morning I didn't know. But if we had waited one more day, we would not have met Alicia. And no telling what might have happened to her walking alone if we hadn't come along. So many people had helped us on the way it felt really good to be able to help someone in return. Maybe that was why I was being pulled out the door in South Fork. Maybe I was needed on the road to Grand Junction. Maybe there were a lot of things going on that seemed like just happenstance that weren't really random chance at all. If that were true, and I certainly was beginning to believe it, I wondered if I would ever be able to figure it out.

We located a campground near Glenwood Springs (campgrounds are all over Colorado), and after a slight struggle we had the tent pitched. John and I had a nice dinner, and we snuggled easily into our nice warm tent. We slept under the stars for the first time in several weeks. It actually felt okay.

Did I mention I liked being kissed by a girl?

CHAPTER 43

JOHN

---

s soon as we were back on the highway the next morning, I noticed Bingo smiling and suspected it was because the sorrow of leaving South Fork was no longer at the forefront of his mind, and we had Alicia to thank for that. At least for the time being. It wasn't long before her memory was replaced with something else. *Thump. Thump. Thump.*

"Dang it! I hope that's just a flat tire we're hearing."

It was.

He pulled over on the shoulder as far off the roadway as he safely could and looked at me. "We might as well get to it."

We got out and I watched as he pulled the jack and spare from the trunk. (I was kind of surprised he remembered it was in the front of the car. I'd forgotten).

"Well whatta you know?" he said. "A full-sized spare!" Actually the Beetle's regular tires were not much bigger than the modern-day donut spares.

While he loosened the lug nuts, I ventured off to pee. (Best to take advantage of every opportunity.) After a short excursion along the fence, I rejoined him.

The jack had never been used and once Bingo figured out its workings, he made short work of the job. He then placed the old tire and jack in the trunk, wiped his hands on his jeans and was just about to open the door when we heard it—an approaching eighteen-wheeler, the driver laying on the horn. He was a few hundred yards down the road coming our direction in the opposite lane. In addition to the horn, the truck's headlights were flashing on and off. We watched curiously as it slowed and squealed to a stop directly across the road from us. The driver jumped out, looked both ways and hurried across the road toward us. He was a big man with a familiar gait. Regardless, I growled and moved in front of Bingo. Then we saw. It was Cliff. From the Big Texan Steak House in Amarillo.

"Well I'll be damned," he exclaimed. "My buddies from Texas."

"Holy cow, Cliff. What're you doing here? How'd you know it was us?"

"Not many cars like yours on the road. Know what I mean? In fact, I'd venture to say yours is the *only* bright yellow, sixties-somethin' VW Beetle roamin' the highways these days."

I remembered hearing somewhere once that there are no coincidences.

"I can't believe it's you," he said. "What are the chances?"

"Well, on the map of Slim and None, I'd say just a tic above None. Or better yet, a speck above. Now let me ask you; what're *y'all* doin' here? I figured you two would have lit somewhere by now."

"Actually we did for a while. In South Fork. We just left there yesterday."

He looked down at me. "John, you're smart enough to

know you fellas can't stay on the road *forever*. So maybe *you* need to pick a place somewhere, put your paw down and tell Bingo enough's enough, you hear?" he chuckled. "Or tell him you're ready to go back home."

I couldn't do *that*.

He looked at Bingo. "Have *you* given any thought to doin' that? I'll bet that mama of yours misses you somethin' awful."

The ever-present lump in Bingo's throat resurfaced. He slowly shook his head. "I can't. As much as I want to, I just can't go back home."

"That's a shame. You don't reckon that asshole dad of yours is hurtin' your mom, do you?"

Bingo's tears were back. "I don't know. I try not to think about it." He paused. "I shouldn't have left her alone there, Cliff. I don't know what I was thinking. I just wanted my own fear and hurt to stop. I know that makes me a coward."

"No, son, it don't. It makes you human. You just needed somebody to stand up for you, that's all. And no one did." The big man stared into the distance, thinking. "What's your dad's name anyway? I don't recall you sayin'."

"Joel Bookman. Why?"

"No reason. Just wonderin'. I'm guessin' you still don't have a phone. Would that be an accurate statement?"

Bingo nodded and Cliff pulled a small notepad and pen from his shirt pocket and scribbled something down. "Well, here's my number anyway. If you ever need anything, you find one and call me. Anytime. You got that?"

"Yes sir."

"Things are gonna work out for you, son. You and John both. One day. You'll see. In the meantime, I have someplace to be and gotta get goin'. You be careful and don't forget what I told you."

"I won't. Thanks for everything."

"You're welcome."

He hugged Bingo and gave me a good, firm head pat-ting. Then he was gone.

CHAPTER 44

JOHN

We got back in the car and it was a minute or two before Bingo spoke. He reached for the map.

"Tell you what, buddy. Even though it's the wrong direction, seeing as how we're this close and may never get the chance again, how about we take a detour through what used to be the Old West? Whatta you say? How do Laramie, Cheyenne and Tombstone sound?"

He wasn't really expecting me to answer, so I just kept quiet. But I must say, the allure of the Wild West grabbed me. Maybe we'd see John Wayne. Or at least where he made some of his movies. Although I was pretty sure the city of Tombstone was in Arizona, not Wyoming.

We continued east toward Denver and though the traffic there wasn't great, it wasn't terrible. We made it through fine and headed north on I-25 toward Cheyenne, arriving a little after lunch. A giant billboard greeted us on the outskirts, proclaiming the city was home to the "Daddy of 'em All—The World's Largest Outdoor Rodeo and Western Celebration", and had been since 1897. We continued on into town, and judging from the packed sidewalks and crowded streets, it was apparent the annual week-long event was, in fact, currently underway. Not being a fan of traffic jams *or* rodeos (Bingo had never been to one but had seen one on TV), he drove on, stopping at the first McDonald's he saw. To my dismay, Bingo was temporarily back on the "keeping me healthy kick". I ate dog food while he enjoyed cheeseburgers and fries. Once we were done and had a potty break, we headed west for Laramie, leaving the crowds behind. An hour later, we were there. Realizing we needed gas, Bingo pulled into a Phillips 66. After he'd gassed the car and paid, he returned with a free pamphlet he'd picked up inside and began leafing through it.

"Dang. This really *was* the Wild West. It says here Laramie's still home to the Bucket of Blood Saloon and the 2nd Street Brothels, although I'm guessing they're no longer in business. And there was even a TV western called *Laramie* at one time, but I don't remember that."

There were several other remembrances of the Wild West scattered about Laramie among the countless restaurants and fast food establishments found in most cities its size. The thought of eating Thai or Sushi here seemed odd, but people clearly did it. Locals mostly, I'm guessing. Bingo decided actual visits to the historical sites would bolster our time-travel experience but chose to push on instead. So we left Laramie and headed north to Casper.

The mountains Bingo had longed for and enjoyed for the past few weeks were gone. This was the epitome of wide open spaces and was actually rather attractive. At least in my eyes. There was the occasional mountain (or tall hill), but those were scattered about few and far between. Just prairie grass and blue sky as far as one could see. We got to Casper around 4:30, and the first thing Bingo did was search out a tire shop to get our flat tire repaired. He found one without much trouble. A young man not much older than

Bingo hurried out to help us.

"Cool car! Where'd you get it?"

"A good friend loaned it to me," Bingo answered as we climbed out.

"I don't know if we have any tires to fit this thing. We might have to order 'em," he said.

"That's okay. I just need a flat fixed. That's all."

"Cool. That, we can do." He walked around to the rear of the car and opened the cover, revealing the tiny engine. Then he looked at us.

"In the front," Bingo said, smiling.

The guy then walked around to the trunk in the front, opened it and smiled. "Well, I'll be. Cool." He removed the flat tire and said, "Give me about ten minutes."

"Take your time," Bingo answered. "We're in no hurry. Come on, John."

We walked down the street to a very nice Best Western motel. A sign on the door told us what we needed to know. "Pets Welcome". He made a reservation and we returned to the shop. Our tire was waiting out front. The attendant returned.

"My boss was really impressed with your car. Said his dad had one like it. Or his granddad, I can't remember."

Bingo smiled and asked, "How much do we owe you?"

"Ten bucks."

Bingo paid, thanked the young man again and we climbed in. The kid walked over to Bingo's window and leaned in.

"He also told me to tell you to let him know if you ever decide to sell it."

"Will do," Bingo replied. He started the engine, and we drove the block to our motel. All in all, Wyoming was okay and our dreams that night weren't half bad.

CHAPTER 45

JOHN

The absence of mountains was weighing on Bingo, I could tell. Many people prefer wide open spaces and relish in them. Bingo does not. I'm pretty sure he feels some sense of security from the feeling of confinement nearby mountains offer, and there were simply none to be found here. After a quick breakfast in our room the next morning of dog food and donuts from the breakfast bar downstairs, we hit the road. Next stop: the Grand Tetons and Jackson, Wyoming.

We got there around 2:00 p.m., stopping only for a quick lunch somewhere along the way. (I can't remember the name of the town; it was pretty small). I don't think either of us was prepared for the Grand Tetons. They are a sight like none other. A breathtakingly beautiful view (yes, even for this dog) unlike anything he or I had ever seen. After ten minutes of staring, we headed south to the town of Jackson to see what it had to offer. Bingo made mention he'd read that lots of famous people hung out there.

Our first stop was at a place called the Bridger Gondola. After brief inquiry inside, Bingo returned, smiling.

"We're in luck. Since there's almost no one here, we can

---

have one to ourselves if we hurry. Come on!"

I excitedly did as I was told and followed him to a small vehicle of some sort hanging from two heavy cables. We climbed in and immediately began moving up the mountain. I wasn't big on the rickety movement and swaying motion. It reminded me too much of our boat ride at Pool Table Lake. Nor was I thrilled about the view. It was a LONG way down. A nerve-wracking twelve minutes later, it was finally over. I jumped out and peed and then followed Bingo over to an observation point. After a minute or two of pay-for-view close-up looks of the Tetons through some sort of a binocular device, he was done. It was sunny and warm back at the car, but that wasn't the case up here. It was cloudy and the wind was howling. I even thought I heard Bingo's teeth chattering—despite it still being August. He spotted an empty gondola returning, and we ran to it. I survived the twelve-minute return trip, peed again and we walked to the car. I was glad to be back on solid ground, and he was happy to be warm again. We settled inside.

"How'd you like that, buddy?"

Boy, I wish I could talk.

We drove south a while, something caught Bingo's eye, and we stopped.

"Oh, man. This will be even better!"

I didn't like the sound of that but hopped out anyway. I walked a short ways and stopped. He was racing toward what appeared to be a scaled-down, cheap version of the last contraption. This one had only chairs hanging from the cables. You can imagine my relief when Bingo dejectedly walked back over and announced, "No pets. Of any kind. Sorry." *Thank goodness.* Better yet, *Thank you, Lord.* We walked back to the car.

It wouldn't start. Bingo tried several times. Then his eyes

grew wide. He looked over at me and smiled. "Out of gas."

We climbed out and a quick visual search from our location revealed no gas stations nearby. We watched a long, black stretch-limousine pull up beside us—its windows dark with tint. A rear window rolled down.

"Need some help, darlin'?"

The voice did not fit the large man seated by the window. He smiled.

"Now I know a good dog when I see one, and that goes for young fellers as well. And I know people in trouble when I see 'em. What can we do to help?"

The voice was coming from inside somewhere, but it was too dark to see. The weird thing was, the voice sounded strangely familiar. Judging from the look on Bingo's face, he was thinking the same thing. Finally, a door on the other side opened and a woman climbed out and walked over. She was short with big blonde hair, bright red lipstick and a smile that could light up the darkest cavern. The sequins on her tight, perfectly-tailored outfit sparkled in the Wyoming sun.

"What's wrong? Cat got your tongue?" And a laugh that could melt the coldest of hearts.

"Dolly?" Bingo managed. "Dolly Parton?"

"In the flesh—although it's saggin' a bit these days." Another laugh.

"What are you doing here?" Bingo asked.

"I have a show to do tonight, that's my excuse. What's yours?"

"Out of gas," he said sheepishly.

"Well that's hardly a mountain to climb. I wouldn't even call it a mole hill, would you, boys?"

Several men in the limo answered, "No ma'am."

"You two have names?"

"Yes ma'am. I'm Bingo and this is John."

She eyed us both and smiled. "Well ain't that a hoot? Ever ridden in a limo?"

"No ma'am."

"Well, come on. Time's a-wastin'. There's gas to be gotten and your chariot awaits." She started toward the car. "Move over, boys. We've got company."

The men did as instructed and Bingo and I climbed in, surrounded by smiling faces. "Find us a gas station, please, Teddy," she called out to the driver. As we pulled away, she introduced us to her band members.

After a short ten minutes involving a quick stop at a nearby station and lots of laughs, we returned to the Beetle and watched as the limo driver poured five gallons of unleaded into it. He then handed the newly purchased empty can to Bingo.

Bingo thanked him and turned to Dolly who had been looking the car over.

"I don't know how to thank you," he said.

"By havin' an early dinner with us, and I won't take no for an answer. We're headed that way right now. All you gotta do is follow."

Dolly was back in the limo before Bingo had time to answer. We jumped in the Beetle and followed it to the Gun Barrel Steak and Game House. Once inside, our group was greeted and led to a small, private dining room. I could see people staring as we walked—probably at Dolly, but possibly at me. I was pretty sure dogs were not allowed in such a nice establishment. Until now, anyway. I straightened my back and walked proud. After Dolly had seated Bingo right next to her, I curled up at his feet.

"Now you can get whatever you want, sweetie, but the trout here is worth orderin' just to see Manny work his magic." Having no idea what that meant, Bingo ordered it out of curiosity. The group munched on an assortment of fried things (mushrooms, pickles, cheese, and green tomatoes) and visited until the main course was served. Dolly saw to it that I received my fair share, and I must say the fried cheese was my favorite.

The head waiter, Manny, set Bingo's plate in front of him. A large, grilled trout accompanied by steamed green beans and home fries. Manny took out two large and very sharp-looking knives and proceeded to swish them about together just above the fish. That's what it looked like, anyway. Then he put the knives away, reached down and removed the fish's bony skeleton in one piece. Bingo's eyes grew big.

Dolly laughed. "I'll bet you've never seen anything like that before."

"Sure haven't. How'd he do that?"

"Only Manny knows. Now just wait till you taste it."

The next hour flew by. Lots of good food and laughter. Dolly did manage to coax Bingo's story from him, but he never cried while telling it. It's hard to cry around Dolly. She just has a way of making things seem better than they really are.

"So what kind of excitement do y'all have planned for tonight?"

"I don't know," he said. "Camping, I guess."

She smiled big. "Well, it's not *nearly* as thrillin' as that, but you two are welcome to come to my show tonight at the Jackson Hole Playhouse if you want. As my personal guests, of course."

"Really? That'd be awesome!"

"OK, then. It's a date!" She then waved Teddy the driver over and whispered something in his ear. He left and returned a few minutes later just as everyone was finishing up a slice of the restaurant's famous cheesecake and handed her a card. She handed it to Bingo.

"Here you go, sweetie. I took the liberty of reserving you and John a room at the Hotel Jackson. I think you'll like it, it's kinda swanky. And don't you worry, John's good to go. He'll likely be the *first* dog ever to stay there, and probably the last, but you won't have any trouble. Trust me. Now the show starts at 9:00, so the band and I gotta get goin'. I need my beauty nap if I'm gonna be standin' in front of a bunch of people tonight under bright lights." Everyone at the table laughed. It was easy to see they all loved Dolly. Who doesn't?

Bingo and I checked into the hotel, not far from the concert. We found our room and stood, staring upon entering. It was like no room we had ever been in before, and we were almost afraid to touch anything—all of the furniture was so expensive-looking and beautiful. I sniffed around while Bingo checked out the fancy bathroom. Pooped, we hopped into the big, cushy bed for a quick nap. When we woke, Bingo took a hot bubble bath in the huge whirlpool tub and shaved. (Like most boys his age, Bingo thought his "beard" was much more prominent than it really was.) He then dressed in his cleanest jeans and one of the nice polo shirts Beth had bought for him. At the last instant he decided to leave me in the room knowing I'm not a big fan of loud music or crowds. And I was good with that. He said goodbye a little after 8:00 and left. It was nearly midnight when he returned. I awoke to find him carrying a beautiful guitar signed by Dolly. He undressed, brushed his teeth and climbed into bed beside me. With his guitar. I wanted to cry at the precious sight of it, but that's not something us dogs do. But we can smile. And when I finally fell back asleep, I was still wearing mine.

The next morning, I heard all about the show, the guitar and Dolly's bus—her home-away-from-home on wheels. Following the concert, she and the band had loaded up in it and headed for Denver. At Dolly's insistence, Bingo and I enjoyed breakfast in our room. This was followed by a warm shower I was unable to dodge (but probably needed). We hung around for a while before checking out (no charge) around 10:00 a.m. Bingo carefully placed everything in the car with the guitar lying gently across the back seat atop the camping equipment. Then we left, feeling good about everything. Dolly has that effect on people. *And* dogs.

CHAPTER 46

BINGO

The events of the night before were still playing in my head. I was amazed by how hard so many people worked to make the concert a success. Guys were moving equipment around, setting up amplifiers, and hooking everything up. The members of the band kept tuning their instruments, making sure that everything was exactly the way they wanted it to be. And nobody worked harder than Dolly. She worked her tail off to make everything look natural and easy and fun. I must admit that when the lights came on, so did Dolly. It was easy to see that she relished the spotlight, and she was in her natural element performing on a stage. All the people around her were so talented, especially the band, and everybody knew exactly what to do at all times. I was awed by the professionalism of everyone involved.

How will I ever do anything that could possibly be cooler than last night? I thought to myself. I thought fly fishing was awesome and going to a ball game was fun, but they were not nearly as exciting as being backstage. How sad it is going to be, I thought, if for the rest of my life I never experience anything as grand as last night. Could the greatest day of my life already be behind me? I thought of all the people cheering and clapping and demanding that Dolly come back out and do one more song. What could life possibly do for an encore after last night?

And then we got to Yellowstone.

Almost immediately we were overwhelmed with things to see. Our necks and our brains could not work that fast. It is a great thing when something is so amazing that it takes your breath away. It is indescribable when something takes your breath away every minute or so.

The first thing we saw was a mama moose with her calf walking right beside the road. She paid us no mind. She was gigantic. John got really excited. He jumped up in the seat and started barking and wagging his tail. He looked pleadingly at me like, "Can I chase them? Please. Just let me chase them!"

Then we saw a big bear walking on all fours about fifty yards away. He rose up on his hind legs and gave us a good stare as we drove by. John's demeanor changed completely. This time the look said, "Don't you dare let me out of this car."

We rounded a curve and there was a herd of buffalo, maybe thirty or forty. I slowed to a crawl. Almost every one of them was bigger than my car! John's look now was simply amazement. I felt exactly the same way. What magnificent creatures. I thought about how these animals roamed and dominated the plains 150 years ago and how they would have easily been masters of some of the land we had just driven through. But times change, sometimes for the good and sometimes for the bad. That is life in a nutshell, I thought—dealing with the good and the bad.

Deer were everywhere. We saw a fox and antelope and ducks and all kinds of birds. We even saw an eagle flying overhead. And a couple of wolves. It was pretty rare to see wolves, and I thought we were really lucky. John did not share my enthusiasm. His look plainly said, "Oh, crap!" But most of the time he was as fired up as I was about all of this. In fact, it would be hard to tell which one of us was having more fun.

Of course, the only thing more exciting than the wildlife was the scenery. I knew the story from school about how President Grant, because of the astounding beauty of Yellowstone, signed a law protecting over two million acres, creating the national park system. My thought as we drove around was hooray for President Grant! We had just witnessed the majesty of Colorado and the Grand Tetons, but I had never seen anything like this. There were beautiful stands of trees and lush grasslands. It was the perfect home for all of this wildlife.

We saw an amazing waterfall. And we saw a little pond or something that had the bluest water I had ever seen, but the banks around it were all red and orange and yellow. Almost all of the ponds had steam rising off of them. There were amazing bluffs and towering hills and crystal clear streams everywhere. *We are doing some fishing today*, I told myself. I had to check out Old Faithful. Sure enough we saw it spew its steam up into the air at least a hundred and twenty five feet. Everybody cheered and snapped lots of pictures.

We drove and drove and looked and looked until we didn't think we could look any more. We found a secluded spot by a fast running stream and pulled over. I set up the tent (it was easier the second time around), unpacked some stuff and then I grabbed my fly rod and we headed to the stream.

John immediately plunged into the water and began

splashing around. "Hey," I told him, "You know the rules. No splashing. It scares the fish." He hung his head and gave me a sheepish look. "Sorry," he seemed to be saying. "Couldn't help myself."

Very quickly I had a really nice trout on the line. I picked him up to let him go. As I looked at him, I thought to myself: You are releasing a great dinner. You have got to get over yourself and learn how to clean fish.

There was another fisherman upstream. Evidently, he had been watching me. He gave a wave and then walked on over. "Looks like you let a pretty good fish go," he said, smiling. "Don't like to eat them or don't like to clean them?"

"I love to eat them. But not clean them."

He laughed. "Easy as pie. Catch another one and I'll show you."

I quickly got another bite. I was able to land it, and we had a nice trout up on the bank. He showed me with his finger exactly where to place the knife to open the fish up and how to remove the head and the skin. He made it look easy. "See?" He smiled again, "Go catch another one and I'll watch you clean it."

He helped me clean a couple of fish. I was starting to get the hang of it. He asked me if I had a good sharp knife of my own I could use, and I said no. So he said he would be right back and took off up the stream.

Soon he was back with another knife and some lemons, garlic, and butter. He gave me detailed instructions on how to cook the trout, and then with a friendly wave he took off to catch his own dinner. Once more, a perfect stranger had stepped in to help us.

That evening John and I enjoyed a nice dinner of pan-seared trout. Sure did beat a bologna sandwich. Thank you, Randy, and thank you, stranger.

CHAPTER 47

BINGO

We slept warm and peaceful in the tent that night, me in the sleeping bag and John curled up against me with a blanket thrown over him. We awoke early the next morning to a chill in the air. We stepped outside the tent, and my breath was taken away again. The sun was just peaking over the edge of the hills around our little stream and everything was covered in dew. Each drop of dew reflected the morning light. It was like walking out in the middle of a million shimmering little pearls hanging on every blade of grass and tree limb. The pale morning light gave the valley a soft glow, and the whole world seemed to be waking up just as we were.

I just stood there for maybe ten or fifteen minutes trying to drink it all in. I looked at John. "One thing is for certain, buddy. Nothing that any person will be able to do or say or build or sing or paint or write will ever be able to hold a candle to God's handiwork. We may never see anything like this again, but it is time for us to be on our way." And with that we loaded up and headed for Kalispell.

The drive was spectacular the whole way. I kept looking around and thinking that Sitting Bull or Crazy Horse might come riding up with a war party at any time. How they must have loved this land. No wonder they wanted to protect it so.

We took our time, occasionally stopping to enjoy dozens of spectacular views.

We visited the National Bison Range and saw even more buffalo. We could have watched them for hours. John especially seemed fascinated by them. He would just stare and stare.

Later we grabbed a late leisurely lunch—another cheeseburger and some dog food mixed with a little left over fish for John. We hit Flathead Lake about 4:00 p.m.

CHAPTER 48

JOHN

The scenic drive along Flathead Lake just south of Kalispell is about thirty miles long, and Bingo never spoke a word. I assumed he was still thinking about our grand visit to Yellowstone but was mistaken. Once the lake was behind us, and we had just five or six miles left between us and town, he opened up momentarily.

"I must be crazy, John," he said. "This is no vacation we're on. I act like it is. Sightseeing. Fishing. I even had us riding a gondola for crying out loud. And the only reason we're here at Kalispell is because I promised Beth we'd come. But what's next? Where do we go from *here?* Where does it *end?*" He then grew quiet again.

When we reached town, he stopped at the first service station we came to and reached into our pile of stuff in the back seat and pulled out the well-worn backpack that'd been with us since the beginning. He unzipped a small pocket, removed Beth's wrinkled, yellow Post-it note and got out and walked inside to ask directions. He soon was back and we were off again. Turns out we weren't that far from Kate's house. A couple of miles and turns later, we entered a pretty hillside neighborhood of quaint, well-cared-for older houses. He glanced at the address again and stopped in front of a small two-story home with white siding and blue shutters around the windows. The blue front door swung open, and a woman came running out. Our initial reaction was, "What is Beth doing here?" It was her—but with grey hair and glasses. We had no sooner stepped out when she grabbed Bingo and hugged him.

"You did come! I was *so* hoping you would! I'm Kate. Beth's sister. But I guess you know that."

We do now, I thought. Bingo still was a little taken back. He stared and said, "Holy cow. Are you two twins?"

"Identical. Except I got Mom's grey hair. *And* her poor eyesight. She looked down at me. "And you must be John. The one and only."

Yep.

She stared at the car. "Oh, and Beth wasn't kidding about the Beetle. My word, I haven't seen one of these in forever."

"Sure beats walking."

"I'll bet it does." She hugged him again. "It is *so* good to finally meet you. Beth has told me so much about the two of you. She was quite taken with you both, you know."

"We feel the same way. She was very special. In a way, she saved us."

"That's what she does. Come in, come in! I have your room all ready. Why don't you go get cleaned up, and I'll order supper. Pepperoni pizza and cinnamon sticks okay? We have a great pizzeria just around the corner."

"Yes ma'am. That sounds great."

Darn sure did. Maybe Bingo would forget and leave the dog food in the car.

"No ma'ams here. I'm Kate. Plain and simple. Got it?"

"Got it."

Kate then showed us to our room and while Bingo show-ered, I explored. I could smell traces of Beth in several plac-es. She had definitely been to visit, but it had been a while. When Bingo was done, we scooted down the stairs toward the smell of hot pizza. I immediately noticed Kate was pre-paring three plates. While they ate theirs at the kitchen ta-ble, I enjoyed my pizza on the floor between them. The dog food remained in the car. When we were done, Bingo said, "Beth said you have something to show me."

"Yes I do. But let's wait until morning for that, if that's okay."

"Sure."

"Right now, how about we move to the living room and relax where it's more comfy? I want to hear all about your journey. It reminds me a little of *Travels with Charley*. Are you familiar with that book?"

Bingo plopped down on the couch and smiled. "I have a copy." I noticed his mood had greatly improved. Either be-cause of the food or Kate. Or both.

"You don't say. I just love the way Mr. Steinbeck wrote, don't you? Maybe you'll be a writer someday. Beth says you definitely have the heart for it."

"I don't know about that. But I do like that book."

Over the next hour, Bingo recounted our entire journey for Kate, focusing on the good parts. "I guess you could say we've been really lucky."

Kate smiled. "You sure it was just luck?"

I can answer that. No. He's not sure, Kate. Far from it.

Bingo thought for a moment and quickly changed the subject. "Are there any of those cinnamon sticks left?" he asked.

"Kate smiled and stood up. "There sure are. How about you, John?"

I barked. Loudly.

She laughed. "Well now, you have quite the vocabulary, don't you?"

If they only knew.

"I think it's the inflection in your voice," Bingo said. "He often barks whenever a question is asked."

"Even so, the best my dogs ever managed was to sit, roll over, shake and annoy the neighbor's cats."

Bingo laughed and if I knew how, I'd have joined him. That was funny. Kate headed for the kitchen, warmed the remaining cinnamon sticks in the microwave and returned. She handed one to me. "Here you go, John."

I gobbled it down and barked.

She looked at Bingo. "*That* wasn't a question."

He laughed. "He'll do anything for food. Trust me."

She spent the next minute or two trying to coax another bark out of me, but I decided enough was enough and kept quiet. Eventually she gave up and began telling us all about Kalispell, nearby Glacier National Park and the Going to the Sun Road.

"What's that?" Bingo asked.

"It's a mountain drive like none other, hon. And definitely not for the faint of heart. Still, everybody should see it at least once. I've heard it described as just a hop, skip and jump from Heaven, and I couldn't agree more."

Bingo looked at me. "We need to see that, buddy."

I wasn't sure. Our car's not that great on mountainous roads.

A minute later they called it a night, and while Kate turned out the lights, we retreated to our room. Sleep came easily, even for Bingo, and was dreamless. I don't think either of us budged all night.

The next morning Bingo made a quick trip to the car

and as a result, I ate dog food while he enjoyed pancakes. Bummer.

"Your pancakes taste just like Beth's," he said with a mouthful.

"Don't ever let her hear you say that. She likes to think she's the only real cook in the family. And the thing is, she's right."

"I promise," he chuckled.

"Now, this thing Beth and I think you should see—I'm ready whenever you are."

He finished his orange juice and said, "Ready!"

We followed Kate out the back door to her garden. It was beautiful. There were flowers I'd never seen before. But she passed it by, stopping just beyond it in the grass. There, before us, stood a skinny little stalk of some sort with a few green leaves and a single white blossom. It wasn't two feet tall.

"This precious little tree dies back every winter but returns each spring, never getting much taller than this. And every year it manages to produce a handful of leaves and a single bloom like the one you see here. One beautiful, fragrant, white flower. You wouldn't know from looking at it, but this is a magnolia tree. In the south, these often grow to be eighty feet tall. They are magnificent. The previous owner brought it with him from Texas. But it's the wrong soil. And definitely the wrong climate. This poor thing doesn't stand a chance here. Still, it chooses to live. And strives to flourish, as best it can. I call it the tree with feelings." She looked at Bingo. "You've never had that chance. Your father robbed you of it."

"How do you know that?"

She smiled. "But you do now. The world is yours Bingo. Yours and John's. And it's a great big world."

"But how do I know where I belong? Where *we* belong?"

Suddenly we heard a familiar voice. *Singing.* Bingo stared at Kate. She smiled and removed her phone from her pocket. The ringtone grew louder. And even more familiar.

"I just love Dolly, don't you?" Kate said, smiling. She then handed Bingo the phone and went inside, leaving us alone with the tree. Bingo stared at the device, then pushed *Answer* and slowly held it to his ear.

CHAPTER 49

JOHN

"Hello? . . . *MOM?*"
Stunned, he walked over and sat in a small chair near the garden. I jumped up into his lap so I could hear.

"Is that really *you?*"

"Yes, Bingo, it is." She was crying. "I love you, Bingo. I miss you terribly. I've been so worried about you."

"I love you too, Mom," Bingo cried. "I miss *you* so much. I'm so sorry I left you there. But I had to. I had to get away. Are you okay? Tell me Dad isn't hurting you. Please say you're okay."

"He's gone, Bingo. Your father is gone."

"What? What do you mean gone?"

"A man driving an eighteen-wheeler showed up here two days ago. A great big fella. He introduced himself as a friend of yours and said you had a problem that needed fixing—one that should have been handled long before now. He forced his way in and Joel went at him with a baseball bat. But the man took it away from him and beat him with it. Hurt him real bad. Then he told Joel to pack his stuff and leave and never come back—or next time he'd kill him and take his time doing it. And the man left. Your father could barely walk, Bingo. Barely move. Then yesterday when I got home from work, he was gone. Along with his belongings. Your father left, Bingo, and I don't think he's coming back. You can come home, you and John. *If* you want to, that is. We can start a new life together. Here, or anywhere you want. Just the three of us."

Bingo was crying hard now. "Of course I'll come home! I've missed you so much. I know John has too." He paused. "How did you know we were here?"

"Kate called me one day. Said she'd gotten my name from her sister in South Fork and that you were headed there to her home in Kalispell. I've phoned every day, hoping and praying that one day you'd be there."

"I can't wait to see you, Mom."

"So you're coming home?"

"*Of course.* We'll be there as soon as we can."

"You be careful, you hear? Drive safely and don't rush. I'll be waiting here for you. I'm not going anywhere."

"I have so much to tell you. You won't believe everything that's happened."

"I can't wait to hear it all."

"And, Mom?"

"Yes, honey?"

"Even if Dad does come back, I'm not afraid anymore. I'm not the same Bingo I was when I left."

"I love you, sweetie."

"I love you, Mom. We're leaving right now."

"Bye, honey."

Bingo hung up the receiver and looked at me, tears streaming down his face.

"You hear that, boy? We're going home."

I barked.

"That was Mom on the phone!"

Two barks.

"You don't mind going back do you? Dad's *gone*."

I should explain that I never learned how to answer in the negative. All I know is yes. I kept quiet.

"So you're okay with going back?"

Loud bark.

"And when we get there, no more back yard for you. You're living inside with us!"

Loud bark. And a swishing tail.

"*And* you can get up on the furniture whenever you want."

Same response. My tail sped up.

He smiled. Then paused, eyeing me closely.

"You love me, John?"

Three loud barks!

"What about Dad?"

A growl. *Come on, Bingo. Keep at it.*

"What about Beth? Like her?"

Loud bark.

"And Kate?"

Loud bark.

"And peanut butter?"

Loud bark.

And beets?

He knew I hated beets. I kept quiet and saw the light bulb go off in his head. *Finally. After all these years!* He paused, disbelieving. Then leaned in close.

"Can you understand me?" he asked softly.

Bark.

"You know what I'm saying?"

Bark.

"Oh my gosh. Are you *talking* to me?"

Three loud barks. The cat was out of the bag.

"Can *all* dogs do this?"

Silence.

"But you can?"

Bark.

"HOLY COW! I—"

Kate came through the back door. She was carrying Bingo's backpack and smiling. "Who was that on the phone?"

Bingo smiled back. "I think you know. Does Beth?"

"Not yet, but she will," she grinned.

I jumped down, and Bingo hugged Kate hard and said, "You and your sister are quite the pair."

"Always have been. I just wished she lived closer. I want her to move to Montana, and she wants me to move to Colorado. I'm guessing someday that'll happen. One or the other."

"I hope so." Bingo looked at me and smiled. "Ready, buddy?" He knew what was coming. A loud bark.

"Sure you don't want to spend another night?" Kate asked. "Get a fresh start first thing in the morning?"

"Thank you, Kate, but I think we're both anxious to hit the road. *I know* we are."

"I know," she said, smiling. She looked at me. "That's some dog you have there."

Bingo and I looked at each other.

"Yes he is," he said, smiling. "He's one of a kind. I guess the Going to the Sun Road will have to wait. But I plan on us coming back someday to visit and bringing Mom. We'll see it then. After a stop in South Fork on the way of course."

"I know Beth would *love* that."

They hugged again, Bingo promised to write and Kate watched from the porch as we walked to the car and climbed in. Bingo started it, fastened his seatbelt, and drove away. As had become our habit, we didn't look back. Heck, even I was about to cry. Just up the road, he pulled into a Shell station with a mini-mart. I jumped out and did my business as he gassed up the car. I returned to my seat just as he was replacing the nozzle. He started inside then stopped.

"You gonna be okay, boy? I'll just be a minute."

I barked a loud yes. He smiled and went inside to pay and returned with a Coke and bottled water for the road. Once in, he retrieved our map from the glove box and studied it.

"You know, with some luck we might make it home in two days. Three tops. How's that sound?"

That sounded great to me, and I let him know with another loud bark. He started the car and looked over.

"Now just because we can carry on a conversation, don't go thinking you have a vote in everything we do. The driver always has the final say, and I don't see you getting behind the wheel anytime soon." And with that he let out a hardy laugh—one I hadn't heard before—and I can't tell you how good it sounded and felt. I barked, he laughed again, and we headed down the road. Toward home.

CHAPTER 50

BINGO

When I left home that late afternoon over a month ago, I thought I was running away from everything. I thought that everyone and everything I knew was better off without me around. I had nothing. Nothing that is, but the best friend that anyone could ever have. It turned out that was really all I needed.

I would have never believed that I was actually running *to* something because I didn't even know that that something even existed. I didn't know that people could be kind and giving and compassionate. I didn't know that a girl, much less two, might find me attractive. And most importantly, I had no inkling at all that I was made of tougher stuff than I ever believed. But I knew these things now.

I also had begun to realize that maybe, even when I was at my weakest, that I didn't have to do it alone. I was beginning to understand that maybe not everything happens by chance; that maybe everything was not just coincidence. Someone told me once there was no such thing. Maybe they were right. And maybe there was somewhere I could turn when I needed help the most.

I pointed the Volkswagen south. I wasn't sure if it could

go that way. It never had with me at the wheel. The map said we had about two thousand miles to get back home. Home, a real home. That is something else that I never knew existed. But I did now.

I had no idea what the road ahead had in store. I wasn't cocky but I certainly wasn't afraid. I believed now that I had inside me almost everything I needed.

And what I didn't have inside me, I had beside me. John—who knew more and understood more than I had ever thought possible. We would be home in a matter of days. And we would be just fine.

EPILOGUE

Well, there you have it. Bingo's story. Or, I guess you could say *our* story. You'll be happy to know Bingo is back in school, making straight A's and is a starting point guard on the boys' basketball team. (I didn't even know he knew how to dribble.) He's also learning to play his guitar, *and* he has a girlfriend—a real cutie named Emily with bright red hair and a level head on her shoulders. Lily and I are both crazy about her. The three of them go to church every Sunday. I have to stay home but am often reminded that *all* dogs go to Heaven.

At Emily's insistence, Bingo finally got a phone of his own. Despite working after school and on weekends at the new Ace Hardware store across town, he still somehow managed to find the time to paint the house inside and out and plant pretty shrubs and flowers all around it. (Joel didn't allow such things.)

Lily is seeing a familiar long haul trucker. He's a big man with a soft heart and a way with words. He's also a problem solver. Needless to say, Bingo and I both approve.

We tried to return Olivia's car to Al, but he wouldn't hear of it. We visit him often. He has a new dog—a Cocker Spaniel named Buster. Sometimes the four of us go for rides in the country in the Beetle, us dogs in the back seat. Buster isn't much of a talker, but that's okay.

Bingo regularly texts and calls our friends from the road.

Mr. Pearson has expanded his oil field business and is now in three states; with the help of his brother, Ed is selling his suncatchers online these days; Doc Worley is running for Mayor; Randy and Sharon have new twin girls; Beth sold her souvenir shop and bought the Mountaintop Bakery; and Kate has her house on the market and is brushing up on her baking skills.

Oh, and Dolly has a new album out called *Life Things*— her first studio album in years. One of the tracks is at No. 18 on the Country Charts with a bullet. (That means it's moving up fast.) The song? *Ode to Bingo*.

As for me, I spend most of my time here on the couch surrounded by my toys, watching TV. I am crazy about old westerns. Bingo bought some new dog food the vet recommended that's supposed to be good for me, and it actually tastes pretty good. Oh, and I am quite the dresser these days. Lily purchased a whole slew of bandanas off the internet for me to wear. There's one for every holiday, as well as the Texas Rangers and Dallas Cowboys. And I must say, I look pretty sharp in them.

Bingo and I talk every day. And no, the girls don't know about my . . . *talent*. Let's see . . . I guess that's about it. The rest, as they say, is gravy. And I love gravy.

John
Dec. 20, 2020

Printed in the USA
CPSIA information can be obtained
at www.ICGtesting.com
JSHW080315031123
51396JS00001B/28